WELCOME TO HORRORLAND
A SURVIVAL GUIDE

ALL-NEW! ALL-TERRIFYING!
ALSO AVAILABLE FROM SCHOLASTIC AUDIO BOOKS

RIDE FOR YOUR LIFE!

GOOSEBUMPS
HorrorLand™
THE VIDEO GAME
NEW FROM SCHOLASTIC INTERACTIVE

NOW WITH BONUS FEATURES!

**LOOK IN THE BACK OF THE BOOK
FOR EXCLUSIVE AUTHOR INTERVIEWS AND MORE.**

NIGHT OF THE LIVING DUMMY

DEEP TROUBLE

MONSTER BLOOD

THE HAUNTED MASK

ONE DAY AT HORRORLAND

THE CURSE OF THE MUMMY'S TOMB

BE CAREFUL WHAT YOU WISH FOR

SAY CHEESE AND DIE!

THE HORROR AT CAMP JELLYJAM

HOW I GOT MY SHRUNKEN HEAD

THE WEREWOLF OF FEVER SWAMP

A NIGHT IN TERROR TOWER

GET MORE GOOSEBUMPS ON DVD!

NEW FROM FOX HOME ENTERTAINMENT

MONSTER BLOOD

A NIGHT IN TERROR TOWER

ONE DAY AT HORRORLAND

RETURN OF THE MUMMY

THE SCARECROW WALKS AT MIDNIGHT

WELCOME TO HORRORLAND
A SURVIVAL GUIDE

SCHOLASTIC INC.
New York Toronto London Auckland Sydney
Mexico City New Delhi Hong Kong

No part of this publication may be reproduced, stored in a retrieval system, or transmitted in any form or by any means, electronic, mechanical, photocopying, recording, or otherwise, without written permission of the publisher. For information regarding permission, write to Scholastic Inc., Attention: Permissions Department, 557 Broadway, New York, NY 10012.

ISBN-13: 978-0-545-09008-7
ISBN-10: 0-545-09008-3

Goosebumps book series created by Parachute Press, Inc.
Copyright © 2009 by Scholastic Inc.

All rights reserved. Published by Scholastic Inc., *Publishers since 1920*. SCHOLASTIC, GOOSEBUMPS, GOOSEBUMPS HORRORLAND, and associated logos are trademarks and/or registered trademarks of Scholastic Inc.

12 11 10 9 8 7 6 5 4 3 2 1   9 10 11 12 13 14/0

Printed in the U.S.A.
First printing, October 2009

"Behind the Screams" bonus material
by Matthew D. Payne

CONTENTS

WELCOME TO

HorrorLand

A SURVIVAL GUIDE

STAGGER INN

Dear Guest,

Welcome to Stagger Inn, the official hotel of HorrorLand! In this binder, you'll find everything you need to ensure an unpleasant, uncomfortable, and truly terrifying stay. We're pleased to be serving you (medium rare, if possible), and promise to make this a visit you'll never forget – whether you're staying a night, a week, or much, much longer.

Sincerely,

Earl E. Grave
Innkeeper

CHeck It Out! Somebody sent us these pages from the official HorrorLand Welcome Guide. But... WHo? Signed, LM1

FAQ's – Freakishly Absurd Questions About Stagger Inn

These are the five questions we get asked over and over again.
We think the answers are a SCREAM!

Q: Is the Inn a REAL castle?

A: Yes and no. The Inn was first built in the mid-1970s along with the rest of HorrorLand. It was designed by world-famous architect Tripp N. Stagger. Tripp wanted his creation to be as authentic as possible, so he had pieces of an actual haunted castle brought over from Eastern Europe. Many of the things you see around the Inn – heavy wooden doors, oil paintings, chandeliers – are from the old castle. Some of the ghosts might be, too.

Q: What are the check-in and check-out times?

A: Check-in is at 4 P.M. We're not sure when check-out is, since nobody's ever checked out.

Q: Why is my shower singing to me?

A: Congratulations, you're in a haunted room! More than half our rooms come with THE GHOSTLY GUARANTEE – our promise that your stay will be interrupted by all sorts of creepy noises and eerie sights – whether it's a singing shower, a floating mini fridge, a ghost sleeping in your bed, or something even WEIRDER!

FAQ's (continued)

Q: Who's the creepy headless guy playing the organ in the lobby?

A: That's just Headless Trevor. Old Headless has been with Stagger Inn since opening day. Nobody knows where he came from. To our knowledge, he's never stopped playing in all those years – not even for one minute. Everyone agrees Headless Trevor is lucky – he can't hear his music!

Q: Why isn't there a mirror in my room?

A: Are you kidding? With YOUR face?

No MIRRORS ? ?

Concierge

Extension 662

HOURS:
Twenty-four hours a day.

The concierge desk is located in the main lobby. Someone is on duty around the clock to help you with:

* Purchasing tickets to HorrorLand's nearly-live shows at the Haunted Theater.

* Obtaining LINE SLASHER passes for our busiest rides and attractions.

* Requesting a taxi from the Last Ride Cab Co.

* Losing your way around the park.

* Finding your way out of your room.

* Finding people (or limbs) you might have been separated from.

I'M ALMOST DONE
DRAWING MAP #1!

In-Room Entertainment

Every room in the Inn comes with a flat-screen TV that doubles as a Web browser (we LOVE webs of all kinds here in HorrorLand). Using your remote control, you can send e-mails, surf the Internet, or just plain watch TV!

Channel Guide

1 Welcome to HorrorLand
A video tour of the park narrated by the one and only HorrorLand MC!

2 Scream-Yourself-Silly Cinema
All the scariest scenes from the scariest movies ever made.

3 The Close-ups of Spiders Channel
Nothing but huge spiders eating flies and crawling over skin.

4 The Cauldron Channel
Cooking shows for slime lovers and worm eaters of all ages.

5 The HorrorLand Hidden Camera Channel
Lowlights from all the episodes of HorrorLand's longest-running series.

6 Dancing with the Squids
Tune in to see live video from our most popular stage show!

7 The Un-Learning Channel
The more you watch, the lower your IQ!

8 The Bad News Network
Nothing but bad news from around the world, 24/7.

9 The Creepy Eyes Staring Back at You Channel
Perfect for falling asleep at night!

10 The Sickening Sports Channel
Everything from zombie wrestling to eyeball eating to quicksand diving!

Gym-nauseum

Extension 664

HOURS:
Midnight – 4:30 A.M.

We usually like our guests slow, and with a little extra meat on their bones. But if you insist on working out, our gym is located on the 10th floor (directly across from the Shock-A-Lot bar vending machine).

EQUIPMENT
Dreadmills
Typical treadmills with two big differences: a hungry alligator chasing after you, and no STOP button.

Munching Bags
These punching bags don't punch back, they <u>bite</u>.

Dead Weights
Nothing builds big muscles faster than lifting super-heavy sea monster bones.

Casket-ball Court
Just like basketball, except the "ball" is a bouncy skull, and the "baskets" are coffins.

Gut Ropes
We've taken traditional jump ropes to a whole new gross-out level!

Hey... I WONDER IF THESE ARE THE SAME COFFINS FROM THE COFFIN CRUISE!

7

Housecreeping

Extension 660

HOURS:
Whenever Linda feels like it.

The Stagger Inn maintains a HUGE housecreeping staff. Actually, it's just Linda – but she's thirteen-and-a-half feet tall!

If you'd like your room made up, just hang the "It's a Sty in Here!" shrunken pig's head on your doorknob. Linda will let herself in – whenever she wants! We guarantee a thorough, top-to-bottom cleaning, including:

Making the Bed
We will quickly replace any dirty, slime-covered sheets with clean, slime-covered sheets.

Emptying the Trash
As a service to the environment, all trash is sent to our restaurants for recycling.

Vacuuming
Our equipment can even handle the oversize bugs that like to nest under your pillow.

Slime-ing Pool and Spooky Spa

Extension 665

HOURS:
9 P.M - 9 A.M.

Located on the dungeon level, our slime-ing pool and Spooky Spa offer guests a chance to unwind after a busy day (or night) of running for your lives. Please note that we're closed during daylight hours to give our pool creatures a chance to rest.

Slime-ing Pool

Our Olympic-size slime-ing pool and yuk-uzzi are housed in a gigantic, dimly lit basement. The yuk-uzzi is filled with a warm, soothing mix of dirty water, ooze, and more creatures than we can count. We're not exactly sure what's in there, but we do know this: Most survivors highly recommend it.

The Spooky Spa

Our world-class staff offers a variety of treatments for the weary traveler:

Spider Massage
Nothing releases back and shoulder tension better than a deep-tissue massage from a giant eight-legged spider. It's like having four massage therapists in one!

Skin Peel

Lay back, relax, and let one of our trained specialists peel off your skin layer by layer. It'll take years off your life...we mean, appearance.

Scream Room

Put on one of our comfy terrycloth robes and have a seat in our warm, wood-paneled chamber – filled with the constant ear-piercing sounds of screaming. How is this relaxing? It feels **SO GOOD** when you leave!

Aroma-scare-apy

Our staff has a collection of scents designed to cause long-lasting panic and dread.

STAGGER INN

Doom Service Menu

Chef Gurgitate's Proud Motto: "EAT OR BE EATEN!"
(Please note: the kitchen is closed from midnight to 6 a.m. for daily
repairs and rounding up of escaped ingredients.)

BREAKFAST

CEREAL......$5
Your choice of Mice Crispies, Dirt Loops, Yucky Charms, or
Cinnamon Scabs (now with more scabs!).

FRUIT BAT SALAD......$4
No one can make a salad out of a fruit bat like Chef Gurgitate.
Served with tangy animal thingies.

THE YOLK'S ON YOU!......$6
A different egg dish every morning—and it's so easy
to pick out the bones!

SQUEEZINGS......$10
Start your day with a tall stack of the chef's famous squeezings,
collected from around the park.

Lunch

(Available 11 A.M. – 4 P.M.)

MUMMY WRAP.........$12

Lettuce, tomato, and salted mummy meat wrapped in delicious bandages!

CHOW VEIN.........$14

A classic dish with a twist. Can you guess what we use for noodles?

MONSTER BLOOD SOUP.........$9

One spoonful, and your problems will seem a lot smaller. So will everything else.

PERSONAL "GRAVESTONE" PIZZA.........$12

Not to be confused with that "other" national brand. Add seventy-five cents for sliced snake bits.

Dinner

(Available 4 P.M. – Midnight)

All entrées are served with your choice of two sides (see below).

FILET OF SOUL.........$19

A prime cut of soul, breaded and served in a delightful coffin-shaped tortilla shell.

FETTUCCINI AFRAID-O.........$14

Pasta tossed in a creamy nightmare sauce.

MESQUITE-GRILLED MOSQUITOES..........$18
Caught daily in our guests' rooms!

SIDES:
Squirrelly Fries, Screamed Vegetables, Black Lagoon Beans, Lice Pilaf,
Mixed Greens, Mixed Reds, and Jelly Jam.

Kid's Menu
(Available All Day)

"CHICKEN" FINGERS..........$8
Animal fingers so good you'll think they're chicken.
Add fifty cents for nail removal.

GROWLED CHEESE..........$7
This sandwich isn't going without a fight!
A favorite among workers at Werewolf Village.

FRANK-FURTER..........$8
Served with relish, mustard, and ketchup.
Has anyone seen Frank the dishwasher?

Desserts

(Available All Day)

BLACK EYE SCREAM.........$6

Traditional ice cream served with a warm scoop of crow eyeballs.

CARAMEL HEADS..........$6

A HorrorLand favorite! Sour shrunken heads coated in creamy caramel.

CREPE SUZETTE..........$8

You'll be dying to know Suzette's secret ingredient. She certainly was.

Beverages

All beverages are $3.

Coffin Coffee
Tea-Rex
Bug Juice
Sour Milk
Bottled Swamp Water

Security

Extension 667

Sorry, but this service is no longer available at the Inn. Too many guards kept disappearing. If you have an emergency, we suggest you exit the Inn and run to the nearest Monster Police station.

Gift Chop

HOURS
Twenty-four hours a day.

Located off the main lobby, the "chop" carries lots of souvenirs from the Inn and other HorrorLand attractions!

T-SHIRTS
"I Staggered Into the Stagger Inn!"

"I Had a Sinking Feeling at Quicksand Beach!"

"I Lost My Head for the Guillotine Museum!"

"The Crocodile Café: You'll Never Eat Anywhere Else!"

"FANGS for a Great Time at the Vampire State Building!"

"I ALMOST Survived HorrorLand!"

"The Coffin Cruise: A Ride to DIE for!"

SOUVENIRS
Miniature Bottomless Canoes
Great for bath time! Each canoe comes with a plastic crocodile, two passenger action figures, and a tube of zombie saliva!

Bat Barn Play Set
Each set comes with a bat plush toy (complete with glowing eyes) and a miniature barn. When you place the bat in the barn, it starts shrieking and flapping its wings!

Doom Slide: The Home Game
A board game based on one of our most famous attractions. Don't be the first player to reach the bottom! A lousy time for the whole family!

No THANKS! THE LAST THING WE WANT IS TO Re-LIVE ANY OF THAT STUFF!

VIDEOS
Dancing with the Squids LIVE!
Our most popular stage show!

The Secret History of HorrorLand
A twelve-hour documentary about all the accidents and disappearances that have occurred at the park since it opened.

Creepy Eyes Staring Back at You
Now you can bring the horror of our scariest TV channel home with you! A full hour of creepiness!

Local Attractions

Don't bother wandering outside the park. Even if you made it over the wall (and we doubt you would), there's nothing within fifty miles of HorrorLand.

IF YOU'RE TRAPPED IN HORRORLAND, DON'T GIVE UP! WE MADE IT OUT, AND SO CAN YOU!

BLACK LAGOON
WATER PARK

GUEST BINDER
SECTION 2:

BLACK LAGOON
— WATER PARK —

If you're lucky enough to survive a night in Stagger Inn, why not reward yourself with a day at the beach? Come discover the most DEEPLY disturbing place in HorrorLand!

After a number of unfortunate incidents, it only seemed fair to warn you about our water park's many thrills (and many, many, MANY dangers). Think of this chapter as your personal life jacket. Now, read up and DIVE IN!

HERE'S THE NEXT CHAPTER FROM THE OFFICIAL HORRORLAND WELCOME GUIDE. I HEARD SOMEBODY SPOTTED ZOMBIE PIRATES IN THIS PART OF THE PARK!
SIGNED, LM1

FAQs – Freakishly Absurd Questions About Black Lagoon Water Park

Visitors are always DYING to find out the answers to these four important questions!

Q: How deep is Loch Ness Lake?

A: Nobody knows. Some parts of the lake are just too deep to be measured. Our scientists have tried every kind of submarine they can get their claws on, but the submarines never reach the bottom (and the crew never makes it back to the top!).

Q: Why do I have to wear those blue rubber shoes on Quicksand Beach?

A: The shoes are made from a special kind of rubber that speeds up the sinking process. Without them, our guests would spend HOURS sinking, and the beach would get too crowded!

Q: Are those REAL sharks?

A: If you mean the ones in the Swim-with-a-Hungry-Shark Ride, then yes! HorrorLand spared no expense flying in the biggest great white sharks, tiger sharks, and hammerhead sharks from across the globe. And after eating so much awful airline food, they're ready for a REAL meal!

FAQs (continued)

Q: What's that smell?

A: That depends on which smell you're talking about! Many of our guests have complained about the smell of Loch Ness Lake. They say it smells like a mix of dirty socks, spoiled milk, and garlic. To be honest, we don't know what causes it. Maybe it's one of the many mysterious creatures that live in the lake. Or maybe it's just the smell of the bottomless pits on Quicksand Beach. Our lifeguards often say, "If it STINKS, it SINKS."

"LIFEGUARDS"?
MORE LIKE DEATHGUARDS!

Loch Ness Lake

Loch Ness Lake was designed by a Scottish engineer named Duncan Waters. He created the lake in the shape of Nessie — the mythical monster from the original Loch Ness in Scotland. Mr. Waters stocked the lake with a rare and colorful species of angelfish, and swimmers found these adorable fish to be quite friendly.

For safety reasons, the lake was dug only ten feet deep. But soon after Black Lagoon Water Park opened, SOMETHING began digging on its own! Today, Loch Ness Lake is filled with piranhas, stingrays, and the seven deadliest species of tortoise. We don't know how these creatures got there. We DO know that they, too, found the angelfish to be quite friendly — and TASTY.

Quicksand Beach

Come relax at Quicksand Beach, where the air is filled with well-fed seagulls and the laughter of sinking children. However, if you're a fan of solid ground, stay home!

The beach is filled with DOZENS of quicksand pits, which aren't always easy to spot. (Here's a hint: If you see an area covered with empty hats, you might want to walk around it.) Lifelike human hands (almost TOO lifelike, if you ask us) and weird animal skeletons stick out of the sand in all directions, making the sight of sinking beachgoers even stranger!

IMPORTANT: Before entering the beach area, all guests must visit the Choose Your Shoes stand and pick up their own pair of blue rubber Sinking Slippers.

I WONDER WHAT HAPPENS TO YOU AFTER YOU SINK!

BLACK LAGOON
WATER PARK

Rules and Regulations

Quicksand Beach

· You must be at least 44 inches tall to sink.
· Do not scream or shout for help. You might disturb other sinkers.
· Animal skulls are NOT souvenirs.
· Be sure to visit the restroom BEFORE sinking.

Loch Ness Lake

· Do not believe rumors. There's no such thing as a man-eating squid.
· If you drink the water, don't swallow the brown lumpy stuff.
· Lifeguards are no longer on duty due to rumors of a man-eating squid.

Water Rides

Hop aboard our four most famous rides and find out why *Dangerous Places* magazine rated our park "The #1 Most Slippery in the World!"

The Swim-with-a-Hungry-Shark Ride

The name says it all! Ever wondered what it's like to be in the middle of a feeding frenzy? Well, wonder no more! One of our helpful Horrors will outfit you in a bite-proof scuba suit, life jacket, and helmet. Next, you'll be smeared from head to toe in extra-stinky fish paste. (This distracts the sharks from our valuable workers.) The rest is up to you!

The Alligator Swimming Pond

Surrounded by a dense manmade jungle, this is the closest thing to relaxation that you will find near Loch Ness Lake. The water's only waist-deep, and it's much warmer than the rest of the lake. This delightful pool of sludge is perfect for swimmers who just want to splash around without getting too tired. But don't splash TOO much, or you'll attract one of the alligators that live there! They're hard to spot in the brown water — that is, until they show you their big white teeth!

The Bottomless Canoe Ride

Another name that says it all! Up to four guests at a time climb into one of our custom-made FLOORLESS canoes! The canoes wind along an underwater track as riders cling to its sides — trying to keep their toes safe from the sharp-toothed sea creatures below!

Water Rides (continued)

The Coffin Cruise

Our oldest attraction — and still one of our most popular! All you have to do is lie back and float along in your personal coffin. That's it. Nothing else happens. Nothing at all.

YEAH RIGHT!
THEY'RE LEAVING OUT
THE PART WHERE THE
COFFIN LID CLOSES AND YOU
GET COVERED IN SPIDERS!

What to Bring

Come prepared. This is no ordinary water park: Things can go wrong at any moment. And if we're doing our job, they will!

We'll provide towels, lounge chairs, and beach umbrellas. Otherwise, you're on your own! Always pack your favorite first-aid kit and a few of the following:

- ## Water-resistant Vampire's Friend brand sunscreen
  Available from 15 to 15,000 SPF.

- ## A change of underwear
  After all, this is HorrorLand, and people DO get scared.

- ## Nose plugs

- ## Ear plugs

- ## Spark plugs
  (The electric eels made us put that!)

The following items are NOT allowed in Black Lagoon Water Park (this means YOU, amateur squid hunters):

- ## Harpoons

- ## Fishing nets

- ## Dynamite

8 Tips for Enjoying Your Day

Don't force a frightened pet to walk on the beach.
(Remember: "If they're scared on land, they'll panic in sand.")

Electric eels can be used to recharge most electronic
devices. Just ask them very politely.

Don't forget to hold your breath after sinking
below the surface.

Arrive early, but not TOO early.
The vampires don't leave until dawn.

Pick a rendezvous point in case you become separated
from your friends or family.

If you become separated from any body parts, you can
reclaim them in the Lost and Found for a small fee.

Don't drink any liquid that doesn't come
in a bottle or can.

Reserve a cabana away from the quicksand pits.
(You want to stay ON the beach, not UNDER it!)

MONSTER POLICE

THE WELCOME GUIDE HAS AN
ENTIRE CHAPTER ABOUT THE
POLICE FORCE?!? WHY SHOULD
A THEME PARK CARE SO MUCH
ABOUT STUFF LIKE COPS AND
X-RAY MACHINES?

SIGNED, LM1

GUEST BINDER
SECTION 3:

MEET THE
MONSTER
POLICE

After a sleepless night at Stagger Inn or an emergen-SEA in Black Lagoon Water Park, some visitors might be under the impression that HorrorLand is "unsafe."

Unsafe? You bet your LIFE it is!

The job of keeping you unsafe belongs to a small group of Horrors known as the Monster Police, or "MP's" for short. Armed with sticky scorpion-snot nets and canisters of toad-vomit spray, they patrol the park in their hideously ugly orange-and-black uniforms.

MP's have always been a part of HorrorLand, but they weren't always called "Monster Police." When the park first opened, they were known as the "Muenster Police." Back then, they targeted misbehaving visitors with spray-canisters filled with moldy Muenster cheese. Also, their uniforms were the same color as, well . . . Muenster cheese.

Thankfully, a young patrolman named Clem Muncie (now Sergeant Clem) realized how silly — and SMELLY — all of this was. He pushed to have the name changed to "Monster Police." In honor of the First Annual Halloween Celebration at HorrorLand, Clem also redesigned the uniforms to match the jack-o'-lanterns in the Haunted Theater. The MP's haven't changed their clothes since!

MP Headquarters

Monster Police headquarters is located directly behind Crocodile Café,
next to Dr. Twisted's Science Lab. It's open twenty-four hours a day,
and there's always a Horror stationed at the front desk — except
when there's something really good on MTV (Monster Television).

HQ is divided into many dark and terrifying chambers.
Here's a brief tour:

The Control Room (Strictly Off-Limits!)

This is the high-tech nerve center that keeps a close eye on every inch
of HorrorLand. From here, the Monster Police can even listen in on your
conversations and tell you when you're getting really boring.

The Detection Chamber

This large room is designed to squeeze the truth out of our guests
— and find any hidden goodies they might be carrying. All Monster
Police are trained to use the different equipment, including the
HEX-Ray Machine, the Groan Throne (if you're asked to take a seat,
DON'T!), and the Spill-O-Tine — guaranteed to make you spill your
guts, one way or another!

The Jail

Who needs a jail? Being in HorrorLand is punishment enough!

How to Get in Trouble in HorrorLand

While we were preparing this chapter, the Guest Relations team took a survey. We asked hundreds of MP's to answer the following question: "What are your favorite reasons for bullying visitors?" Below are the three most popular answers. Don't say we didn't warn you!

Reason #3: Monster Blood
Due to a recent event at the Hungry Crocs Piggyback Ride, anyone caught with Monster Blood will have to eat it. And then you'll be in BIG trouble!

Reason #2: Meddling
"Some things are nobody's business but ours," said Sergeant Clem. "Why? BECAUSE WE SAID SO!"

Reason #1: Mirrors
"No mirrors of any kind are allowed," said an officer named Benson. "It's for your own safety, really. You don't want to see what you look like after one day at HorrorLand."

ARRESTED?
JUST BECAUSE OF A MIRROR?!!
WEIRD!

Remember Your Rights

In HorrorLand, your rights are easy to remember: You don't have any!

However, the Monster Police reserve the right to arrest, trip, slap, swat, or pinch any guest at any time. If you are put in jail, they also have the right to remain violent, the right to unleash spiders when they question you, and the right to feed you no more than once a year during your stay!

The following news announcement was sent to:
*GRIME Magazine, Oozeweek, Scary People Magazine, Pox News, The Sludge Report,
The Washington Ghost, The Associated Mess, The New York Slimes,* and *BNN*
(Bad News Network).

"Sorry About the Hungry Crocodiles!"

We at HorrorLand were shocked and disgusted — and not in a
fun way — by the unfortunate "incident" that recently took
place on the HUNGRY CROCS PIGGYBACK RIDE.

We realize that everyone loves crocodiles, but not crocodiles
ten times their normal size. On behalf of everyone here at
HorrorLand, the Monster Police would like to apologize to all
the guests who were involved in the, uh, *situation* — especially
those guests who were eaten more slowly than others.

Fortunately, the giant crocodiles were finally defeated by an
equally giant plant. Unfortunately, the plant also attacked
several guests, and it's still on the loose!

"After reviewing the evidence, we strongly suspect that the

entire incident is related to a mysterious green ooze called Monster Blood," said Officer Howard U. Likeapunchindanose. "This incident only goes to show you why Monster Blood is ILLEGAL in HorrorLand!"

Thanks to Officer Howard's detective work, no Monster Police were harmed that day.

HOW did the green goop get inside the park? Apparently, genuine Monster Blood somehow ended up in the popular Monster Blood Soup served at the Crocodile Café. (Usually, Chef Gurgitate uses a homemade imitation.) WHO — or WHAT — was responsible? The kitchen staff claims they don't know, but the Monster Police are launching a full-scale investigation into this event.

They are also looking into another recent sighting at Dr. Twisted's Science Lab.

For more information, contact:

Lou Tenant
Chief of Monster Police

39

ZOMBIE PLAZA

Something VERY scary ahead
on page 7 of this chapter!

SIGNED, LM1

GUEST BINDER
SECTION 4:
ZOMBIE
PLAZA

If you're not too busy running from the Monster Police, run over to Zombie Plaza — the shopping and entertainment center of HorrorLand!

Zombie Plaza is packed with all kinds of stores, arcades, booths, street shows, and, of course, the world-famous Haunted Theater. You'll see kids holding black balloons, Horrors juggling skulls for your entertainment, hungry shoppers wolfing down Monster Dogs — maybe even hungry MONSTERS wolfing down shoppers.

So put on your walking shoes and bring your MUMMY — oops, we mean MONEY!

SHOP TILL YOU DROP!

Some of our guests come to Zombie Plaza empty-handed and perfectly calm, but none of them leave that way! That's because we have the finest, scariest shops in all of HorrorLand.

Gloomingdale's

Five floors of the gloomiest clothing, cosmetics, and home décor you can imagine — from toad-skin sofas to black wedding dresses. Don't miss the Miserable Makeover department, where experts will transform you into a depressing diva!

BOO-Jeans

Every pair is custom-made by an in-store team of ghosts and pre-stained with a secret blend of slimy ingredients. Guaranteed to fit you tighter than 1,000 leeches clinging to your skin!

Cornelia's House of Unpleasant Odors

Spray cans filled with HorrorLand's grossest smells! Now you can "freshen" your home with the stench of Loch Ness Lake or the sweet smell of the dungeon beneath Stagger Inn!

Radio Shriek

Gadgets to make you scream with delight! The Shriek has all the latest toys and electronics, like Robotic Dancing Squids, Sharptooth Headsets, Radio-Controlled Bottomless Canoes, and EYE Pods!

Snot Topic

"You want it? Snot a problem!" Every snot-themed product you can imagine is under one roof, from candies to souvenir pillows — even jars of monster boogers in every color of the rainbow. Bring a tissue!

Old Gravy

They sell one thing and one thing only — jars of homemade gravy that have been left out in the sun for a week. Why not take some home for your next Thanksgiving? We guarantee your guests won't overstay their welcome!

Tear-A-Bear

Start with a cuddly, dressed-up teddy bear, and then rip it apart till it's nothing but fur and stuffing! Each bear comes with a commemorative carrying-coffin and framed "before and after" photo.

GRAND OPENING:

MAKE A FACE!

MAKE A FACE is Zombie Plaza's newest store, featuring hundreds of hideous masks that are so real they're scary! Each one is handmade by Morgana the Master Mask Maker using her own top-secret ingredients. She won't tell us what those ingredients are — all we know is, she's never asked for any rubber, paint, or fake hair.

Be sure to visit the Kids Corner in the back of the shop for the most realistic "masks" of all! Who knows? If she likes the way you look, Morgana might even add YOU to the permanent collection!

MEET
MADAME DOOM

Every day in Zombie Plaza, people line up at a popular booth featuring the mechanical fortune-teller known as Madame Doom. She's pretty wise for a wooden dummy: Her predictions always seem to come true!

Nobody knows all of Madame Doom's secrets, but here are a few details about her mysterious past: Before HorrorLand was built, the park's founder traveled the world in search of scary things to inspire him. In Russia, he visited a dusty old warehouse and found several Madame Doom booths hidden under a pile of junk — where they'd been for fifty years.

According to local legend, there was once a fortune-teller named Clarissa the Crystal Woman. She used to travel from village to village reading palms, and it was said that her predictions always came true. One day, she read the fortune of a young inventor named Ivan. She predicted that he would die heartbroken and poor. Ivan was so angry at her prediction that he threw Clarissa off a cliff and into the ocean!

So Ivan built his own fortune-telling machine. He hoped it would give him a happier prediction. But the little wooden fortune-teller kept saying the same thing: "You will die heartbroken and poor." Ivan spent all his money building five more Madame Doom machines, but each time, he got the same answer.

The legend says that he died of a broken heart soon after.

Some people think that Clarissa's spirit became trapped inside the machines, and that Madame Doom's voice is actually her voice speaking from beyond the grave. We're not sure if that's true. All we know is that Madame Doom always tells the truth. Be sure to pay close attention if she ever has advice for YOU.

And if she offers you a fortune-telling card with no writing on it at all . . . beware. It means you have no future.

Oh, no! We got a card like that in the mail! But WHO sent it???

THE HISTORY OF THE
HAUNTED THEATER

Everybody knows that the Haunted Theater is the best place
to see live entertainment in HorrorLand. But did you know it's
also the best place to see DEAD entertainment?

When HorrorLand needed somebody to build its horrifying
theater, the first — and only — volunteer was a magician
named Mondo the Magical. Mondo designed a theater that
was long and narrow. He said this would force people to
keep their eyes on the stage — even if they were scared
and wanted to look away. He also covered the seats in white
fabric so they would look like an army of little ghosts! For
the finishing touch, Mondo decorated the walls with pictures
of screaming park guests.

When it finally opened in 1981, some very strange things
started happening, like the evil laughter that filled the
theater before every show. At first, everybody thought it
was coming from the hidden speakers in the walls. But when
they looked, they saw that the speakers hadn't been plugged
in yet! Strangely, people were seeing ghosts all over the
place. Ghosts even began helping out around the theater
— for free! (It turned out that ghosts don't have much use
for money.) In 1986, it was named the Haunted Theater in
their honor.

THE
HAUNTED THEATER

Get ready for another year full of SPIRITED events and GLOWING reviews!

Please—No BOO-ing in the auditorium!

OCTOBER 31:
Annual Pumpkin Food Festival

The year begins on Halloween! Join us at midnight for pumpkin-flesh brownies, pumpkin-seed soup, and pumpkin drops. How do you make a pumpkin drop? Toss it off the roof!

NOVEMBER 9–16:
The Dance of the Invisible Spiders

You've never seen one hundred spiders dance like this before. And you never will!

NOVEMBER 27:
All-You-Can-Eat Turkey Dinner

Let our turkeys eat all they can—or you might get GOBBLED.

DECEMBER 17–21
A Very Hairy Christmas

HorrorLand's original HOWL-iday show! All the parts are played by werewolves, from the sharp-toothed reindeer to not-so-jolly St. Nick! Santa's CLAWS are coming to town!

FEBRUARY 25–28
Zombies on Ice

It's our job to make these events sound exciting, but we'll be honest with you — this is the worst show of the season. All the zombies do is fall down, get up, and fall down again. Who thought this was a good idea? Zombies can barely walk!

MARCH 15–22
Vampire Comedy Tour

People don't think vampires are funny, but they're actually a bunch of cut-ups! Don't miss all of the funniest vampire jokes like "What's a vampire's least-favorite food? Stake!"

JUNE 4–10
The Belch Boys

Live in concert, belching out all of their classic hits like "Bad Vibrations," "Burping Safari," and "Belchin' USA." The Boys guarantee at least 1,000 stinky burps a night, so nose plugs are highly recommended.

JULY 3–7
Squids: The Musical!

From the producers of "Dancing with the Squids," this brand-new extravaganza features catchy songs like "If I Had a Face, I'd be Smiling," "Let's Hold Tentacles," and "Oops...I Inked."

AUGUST 10
Mondo's Night of Waaay Too Many Snakes

HorrorLand's favorite magician returns, and this time he's locking himself in a glass box filled with 1,000 poisonous snakes. We're not sure what's "magic" about that, but we can't wait! ONE NIGHT ONLY.

WEREWOLF VILLAGE

GUEST BINDER
SECTION 5:

WEREWOLF
VILLAGE

Welcome to Werewolf Village!

Werewolf Village is weird, even by HorrorLand standards. That's because it's the only attraction in the whole park that's also a real, working neighborhood — where real werewolf families live, play, and eat (and trust me, you don't want to be around when they do!).

Each day when the park opens, the locals are nice enough to let HorrorLand guests into their backyards — and most of the time, they're nice enough to let them out! So if you've got the guts (and they're still on the inside), come and check out what living like a werewolf is really like!

Just make sure you don't "Were" out your welcome!

Regards,
Ima Sheepeater
Director of Werewolf/Human Relations

History of Werewolf Village

When HorrorLand first opened, all of the Horrors lived together in a nearby apartment building. Many of them even shared rooms. A vampire might have a zombie roommate; a dancing squid might share a room with a mummy — everything was fine. That is, until the morning after the first full moon. Anybody who had been sharing a room with a werewolf disappeared!

The owners decided it was too dangerous to let the werewolves live with the other Horrors, so the idea for "Werewolf Village" was born. A spot was chosen on the east side of the park, next to the woods (now known as Wolfsbane Forest). For the first few years, the village was strictly off-limits to guests. But the owners realized what a cool attraction it would make, so they added some shops, a petting zoo, and a path through the dense forest so guests could find their way out.

For the most part, the werewolves get along with their human visitors — as long as they stay out of forbidden areas and leave the village by sunset. Remember . . . HorrorLand can't be held responsible for what happens in Werewolf Village after dark.

"Mane" Attractions

We might not have as many shops as Zombie Plaza, but we have the only shops where you can get up close and personal with real werewolves – close enough to smell the raw meat stuck between their fangs! Each shop is tucked away in its very own creepy cottage.

Make Me Howl!

Ever wonder what you would look like as a werewolf? Using our own special cameras and computers, we'll take your face and transform it right before your eyes — stretching your nose into a snout, covering you with fur, and stuffing your mouth with digital fangs. Each guest gets a framed print of their howling alter ego!

Moment of Paws

A spa and salon that's 100 percent staffed by werewolves! Not many people know this, but werewolves love massages, since all that transforming between human and wolf puts a strain on their muscles. They're also experts at shampooing, blow-drying, and giving haircuts, since, well . . . they're covered in hair.

Wolfgang's Music Shop

As far as we know, this is the only place in the whole world where you can buy recordings of real werewolf howls. Wolfgang's also features a whole section of "moon-themed" music and a daily in-store performance by "Howie and the Howlers" — the most popular all-werewolf band on the planet!

Fur Sure!

Stylish clothing, handmade by werewolves from their own hair trimmings! Where else can you get an incredibly itchy T-shirt, pair of slacks, or riding cape made from grade-A werewolf fur? Each garment is guaranteed to last one hundred moon cycles and comes with an overpowering smell of "damp forest" that never washes out!

Over the Moon Souvenirs

Make your trip to Werewolf Village last a lifetime (unless you'd rather forget it). They have "I RAN Through Wolfsbane Forest" T-shirts, silver bullet key chains, wolf cub dolls, miniature Werewolf Village play sets, jars of authentic werewolf drool, wolf's tooth necklaces, and much more!

Wolf It Down

If you're hungry in Werewolf Village (and you don't have fangs), there's only one restaurant to choose from — and it doesn't have meat on the menu! Most werewolves eat nothing but REALLY fresh meat, but Wolf It Down was started by a small group of werewolf vegetarians who refuse to eat humans for health reasons.
Some of their most popular dishes are:

ONE-ARMED SHEPHERD'S PIE
(with tofu-based lamb substitute)

CUB CLUB CHEESE SANDWICHES

"LITTLE PIGS LETTUCE IN" SALAD

THE WEREWOLF PETTING ZOO

It's the most popular part of the whole village — where human kids can snuggle fluffy gray wolf cubs and pet some of the bigger werewolves, too (if they're brave enough).

Our petting zoo is a little different than the ones you're probably used to. Instead of a waist-high fence to keep the animals in, we have a twenty-foot electrified steel cage. Instead of machines that give out handfuls of food pellets, we have machines that give out handfuls of raw meat, which guests feed to the wolves on the end of long poles. And instead of cute, cuddly goats and sheep eating out of your palm, there's a good chance these animals will eat your palm!

PETTING ZOO RULES:

- Do NOT carry raw meat in your pockets — trust us!
- Please don't collect wolf droppings as souvenirs. That's just gross.
- No playing "fetch." They aren't dogs, they're werewolves.
- Do NOT tease the bigger, caged werewolves — we're not sure how strong those cages are.
- Please don't use the electric fence to recharge your cell phones.

Wolfsbane Forest

After dark, the werewolves leave their cottages behind and head into Wolfsbane Forest to hunt for food. Even during the day, the thick, tall trees block out most of the light, making it seem like night. The tree trunks are crawling with big bugs, and hungry creatures wait in the shadows, including the rare white wolf — a distant cousin to our werewolves, only not as friendly to humans. It's almost never seen, and when it is, the person who sees it usually doesn't live to tell about it!

The forest is a really, really scary place. So scary that the workers in charge of trimming all of HorrorLand's trees and bushes refuse to go in (which lets the thick forest grow even thicker). When Werewolf Village opened to the public, we made a short path into Wolfsbane Forest so guests could explore it without getting lost. Before entering, each guest is given a flashlight and a wolf-shaped digital timer. The timer howls when the sun is about to go down — which means it's time for you to get out!

Unfortunately, some guests don't stick to the path. Which brings us to the one and only rule in Wolfsbane Forest:

STICK TO THE PATH!!!

If you're crazy enough to wander deeper into the forest, chances are, you'll never be seen again (not in one piece, anyway). And even if you do make it . . . you might not like what you find out there.

The Silver Bulletin

EXTRA!

DR. MANIAC SPOTTED IN HORRORLAND!

by Harry Knight, Cub Reporter

WEREWOLF VILLAGE — HorrorLand officials are keeping their lips sealed, but *The Silver Bulletin* confirms that Dr. Maniac has been spotted in the park as recently as this morning!

"He was just bouncing all over the place," said a Monster Police officer who wished to remain anonymous. "He kept babbling about some nutty ice show and some kid named Ronnie . . . or maybe it was Robby."

Dr. Maniac — who wears a leopard-skin cape, yellow gloves, and yellow feathered boots — was first spotted around ten a.m. jumping out of a large video screen in Zombie Plaza. As frightened shoppers ran for cover, they heard him yell, "I'm as free as a flamingo in an opera house!" before disappearing with a loud pop.

When we tried to contact HorrorLand's offices for a comment, all we got was this recording: "HorrorLand has no idea what you're talking about. Everything is fine. Stop calling us."

Dr. Maniac has also been spotted throwing snowballs off the roof of Stagger Inn, trying to freeze all the water in the Bottomless Canoe Ride and building an igloo near the entrance to Werewolf Village. Werewolf officials are urging every man, wolf, and cub to stay inside their cottages until further notice.

"I don't know where he came from," said Stagger Inn's Linda the Cleaning Lady, "but he sends a chill down my spine. And that's not easy to do, since my spine is about eight feet long."

RIDERS SPEND HOURS STUCK ON BOTTOMLESS CANOE RIDE
by Wolf Blister

BLACK LAGOON WATER PARK — About twenty guests got more than they bargained for when they climbed into their canoes this morning. Instead of the usual terrifying trip down a man-made river, they sat for hours — freezing their bottoms off in blocks of solid ice created by Dr. Maniac. It took rescuers hours to reach the stranded . . .

RIDES & ENTERTAINMENT

ESCAPE

www.EnterHorrorLand.com

GUEST BINDER
SECTION 6:
RIDES &
ENTERTAINMENT

When HorrorLand first opened in the 1970s, it had less than ten rides. Some of them were VERY dangerous, like The Tunnel of Broken Glass. Others were just plain crazy, like The Unfinished Roller Coaster – which was shut down after one day and never reopened.

But that was a long time ago. Today, HorrorLand has some of the biggest, most advanced, and scariest rides ever built. For thirteen years in a row, we're proud to have more puking riders than any park in the world*. We're also proud of our improved safety record: last year, we passed almost 10% of our inspections!

And if you're too dizzy (or too scared) to ride, we also have some of the coolest, freakiest arcade games ever created. So pull down your lap bar, or pop in your token, and get ready to SCREAAAAMMM!

Rusty Boltz
Director of Rides and Entertainment

*According to B.A.R.F. – The Big Association of Ride Fans

THE
TOP TEN SCARIEST RIDES
IN HORRORLAND

10. Hungry Crocs Piggyback Ride
They're lean, green, and extremely mean.

9. Bottomless Canoe Ride
Looking for safety? Don't hold your breath!

8. Landmine Maze
Watch your step. Victory will be yours . . . or MINE!

7. Coffin Cruise
Why not go with the flow? Lie back and relax. Forever.

6. R.I.P.P.E.R. Dipper
The fastest one-way bumper car ride, with the biggest BUMP!

5. The Doom Slide
Trust us – this is one slide on which you DON'T want to reach the bottom.

4. The Splat-O-Pult
Flying through the air? Easy. Landing? Not so easy.

3. Scary-Go-Round
A new "spin" on a classic ride. Hold on to your stomach!

2. Swim-with-a-Hungry-Shark Ride
Can you make it across in one piece? Or even two pieces? We doubt it.

1. The A-Nile-Ator.
This roller coaster is so scary, you'll be screaming for your mummy!

HOW TO TREAT A VIP
(VERY IRRITATING PERSON)
TIP #1

All humans are annoying, but SOME (especially the younger ones) are such a PAIN that they deserve "special" levels of fright. Here's a tip from your fellow employee:

TIP: "If a couple of humans get on my nerves, I loosen a few of the bolts on their Fear-Is-Wheel or A-Nile-Ator car. The extra shaking and rattling usually scares them so badly that they don't talk for a week. And as my grandpa used to say, 'The only good human is a quiet human.'"

Grock Wartnose
Ride Mechanic

HORRORLAND'S RIDE RATINGS

Next to every ride in HorrorLand, you'll see a sign with one of these symbols on it:

They stand for "Lose Your Voice (from screaming)," "Lose Your Shoes," and "Lose Your Lunch." It's an easy way to know if the ride you're about to get on is scary, REALLY scary, or so-scary-I'll-never-get-on-another-ride-again scary!

Here's an example of one of our favorite rides from each rating:

Bottomless Canoe Ride

Up to four riders remove their shoes and socks and climb into a canoe that's been coated with gooey grease. You wind along an underwater track through a dark, dense jungle – until suddenly, the floor of the canoe falls away! As you try to cling to the slippery sides, all kinds of slimy, hungry, razor-toothed sea creatures jump and snap at your toes! As if that's not scary enough, high-tech motors tip and shake the canoe when you least expect it! Can you hold on long enough to avoid becoming fish bait?

Rating:

The Splat-O-Pult

One at a time, riders strap on a bicycle helmet and a pair of goggles and climb into the bowl of a giant catapult (located between the Vampire State Building and Mind Swamp). On the count of "two," they're launched hundreds of feet into the air, getting an incredible vulture's-eye view of the whole park. When things go according to plan, they land in a swimming pool full of stale pudding on the other side of HorrorLand, creating a delightful "splat" noise. When things don't go according to plan, the "splat" isn't so delightful.

Rating:

The A-Nile-Ator

There's no doubt about it – this is as scary as roller coasters get! You lie in your own mummy case, which slowly rolls to the top of a giant yellow pyramid. When gravity takes over, you're spun, whipped, and flipped around – with no safety bar to hold you in place! Round and round the pyramid you go, so high above the ground that Horrors look like purple-and-green ants! And just when you think it can't get any worse, your mummy case begins to turn upside down, trying to dump you out!

Rating:

THREE ANCIENT EGYPTIAN CURSES
(AND HOW TO AVOID THEM)

When we built The A-Nile-Ator, we wanted it to look and feel like a piece of ancient Egypt. So instead of building it with fake plastic statues, mummies, and pyramids, we brought the real things over! Unfortunately, we also brought over some ancient curses, too. As a courtesy to our guests, we've provided a guide to avoiding and curing them:

THE CURSE OF THE MUMMY'S BREATH
A curse that slowly turns humans into mindless mummies.

How to avoid it: Easy – never get close enough to a mummy to smell its breath!

How to cure it: The only cure is drinking an entire bottle of squid tears. And as everybody knows, squid tears taste like a mix of sour milk and sewer water.

THE CURSE OF THE SPHINX STATUE
A curse that guarantees a person will have
nothing but bad luck for thirteen years.

How to avoid it: Never, EVER look at HorrorLand's Sphinx Statue for
more than thirteen seconds in a row!

How to cure it: The Sphinx Statue curse can be reversed by climbing
up the statue's head and kissing its nose thirteen times in a row. Of
course, you'll have to do it with your eyes closed — otherwise you'll
just get the curse all over again!

THE CURSE OF THE SEVEN SNAKES
A curse that causes seven small snakes to come out of
a human's mouth every time she or he speaks.

How to avoid it: We're not sure, but we think this curse affects people
who lick The A-Nile-Ator's pyramid. So for the record ... DON'T LICK
THE A-NILE-ATOR'S PYRAMID!

How to cure it: Unfortunately, the only way to cure this curse is by
swallowing a live mongoose.

HOW TO TREAT A VIP
(VERY IRRITATING PERSON)
TIP #2

All humans are annoying, but SOME (especially the younger ones) are such a PAIN that they deserve "special" levels of fright. Here's a tip from your fellow employee:

TIP: "If a human gives me a dirty look, I'll secretly drop some raw steak into his shopping bags or pockets. Then I'll give him a coupon for a 'free dinner' in Werewolf Village (what I don't tell him is that HE'S the free dinner!). As soon as the werewolves smell that raw meat, they go CRAZY and attack! It's hilarious!"

Deena Drool
Director of Kitchen Cockroaches

BEHIND THE SCREAMS: EMPLOYEE RIDES AND RELAXATION

Being around humans is very stressful for our employees. Not only do humans look, sound, and smell weird, but certain human behaviors (like smiling) can drive Horrors to the brink of insanity – or beyond. After hundreds of "stress-related employee attacks" on our guests, HorrorLand decided to create a program to A) help Horrors deal with their stress and B) educate them about human behaviors.

The Horror Relaxation Room

Located next to the Landmine Maze, the Relaxation Room is a private oasis where Horrors can gather and unwind after a stressful day of dealing with humans. They can watch live videos of screaming humans (from rides all over the park), trade tips on making HorrorLand a living nightmare for the guests, and enjoy octopus cakes and cans of bat drool from the vending machines. It's also where we post our Horror of the Month award, for the employee who's made the most guests miserable!

Human Simulation Training

Before they can work in the park, Horrors have to complete H.S.T. – a program designed to help them understand the strange world of humans. The training takes them through a "normal" human day: brushing their teeth (weird), eating cooked food (really weird), and driving a car around HorrorLand's parking lot (this might explain some of the "unexplained" dents on your car). For most Horrors, it's the first time they've ever done ANY of this stuff!

HOW TO TREAT A VIP
(VERY IRRITATING PERSON)
TIP #3

All humans are annoying, but SOME (especially the younger ones) are such a PAIN that they deserve "special" levels of fright. Here's a tip from your fellow employee:

TIP: "If humans give me lousy tips for carrying their luggage, I do a few things to pay them back: First, I go to the Inn's basement and switch their shower pipes from 'hot water' to 'cold slime.' Second, I tell our housecreeper, Linda, to put extra spiders in their sheets and pillowcases. Last but not least, I make sure that crocodiles 'accidentally' find their way into their bathtubs."

Ray Scar
Stagger Inn Bellboy

THE PLAY PEN GAMES & PRIZES

The Play Pen is HorrorLand's arcade, featuring state-of-the-art video games and classic carnival games side by side — all specially designed and built for us and nobody else! In fact, everything in The Play Pen is one-of-a-kind: from the skull-shaped tokens to the ooze-coated prize tickets!

NEW ARRIVALS!

SCARE HOCKEY

What do you get when you mix air hockey with a puck that bites? A bunch of Band-Aids and a ton of fun!

4 Tokens:

VIRTUAL A-NILE-ATOR

Too scared (or smart) to ride the real one? Climb into this fully automated simulator instead! We guarantee all the thrills with none of the spills!

8 Tokens:

LANDMINE PINBALL

It's just like every other pinball machine you've ever played — until you hit the wrong bumper! We go through five of these machines every week!

3 Tokens:

NEW PRIZES!

GLAMOROUS GOBLIN PRINCESS KIT

Finally, the beauty secrets of little goblin girls are yours! Each kit comes with a crown, fake warts, press-on claws, frog-sweat breath spray, dazzling goblin lipstick, and eyeball shadow! You'll be the prettiest human in HorrorLand!

DANCING SQUID PLUSH DOLLS

Just like the Squids in HorrorLand's most popular live show, with realistic "tentacle shaking" action! The perfect dance partner or snuggle buddy for bedtime! (batteries not included)

REMOTE CONTROL BAT

These little critters soar and swoop just like the real thing! Each bat comes with a wireless controller, authentic flapping wings, glowing red eyes, and bloodsucking fangs! (bandages not included)

MONSTER
RESOURCES

ESCAPE
~~www.Enter~~HorrorLand.com

GUEST BINDER
SECTION 7:

MONSTER RESOURCES

HorrorLand is always looking for some new blood (preferably green) to operate our rides, work in our shops, or just hang around making nasty faces at our guests. If YOU'RE a monster looking for a career in the fast-growing Scare Services industry, please print out this form and send it to me care of HorrorLand's Department of Monster Relations. One of our headhunters will contact you if we have any positions available—or if he just likes the look of your head.

Les Chompem
Director of Monster Resources

HELP WANTED
MONSTER JOB APPLICATION

Personal Information

Name _____

Height_____ Length of Horns _____ Length of Tail _____

AIN (Antisocial Insecurity Number) _____

Which of these creatures do you look like? Circle one.
- A – A giant insect
- B – An octopus
- C – A Komodo dragon
- D – All of the above

On a scale of 1 to 5, how ugly are you? Circle one.
- 1 – A little ugly
- 2 – A lot ugly
- 3 – Traffic-stopping ugly
- 4 – So ugly that other monsters call me ugly
- 5 – Too ugly to work anywhere else

Which of these smells most resembles your breath? Circle one.
- A – Raw onions
- B – Garbage on a hot day
- C – That thing at the bottom of your locker
- D – Other (please describe)

Salary Requirements

Salaries depend on your level of experience and the type of job you're hired for. Please look through the list below and circle the currency you'd like to be paid in, and how many pounds per week you require. (Sorry, but due to new HorrorLand regulations, we can no longer pay our employees in humans.)

Toenail clippings
Rotting meat
Live maggots
Hamster steaks
More of that thing at the bottom of your locker

Employment History

Have you ever interacted with humans before?
Yes   No

If "yes," did you find the experience to be (circle one):
A – Terrifying
B – Confusing
C – Delicious
D – All of the above
E – Other (please describe)

Special Skills

We're always looking to take advantage of our employees—especially those with special skills that might help us provide guests with an even more terrifying stay. Please list any special talents you have that might be useful at HorrorLand. A few examples:

Vampire dentistry
Cooking with stale ingredients
Piranha grooming

Spying on humans
Collecting and smashing mirrors

Education

Highest level of schooling:
    A – Monstergarten
    B – Fright School
    C – Monster College
    D – School of Hard Knocks

What was your score on the M.A.T.'s (Monster Aptitude Test)?
        0 – 250 (Not That Scary)
      251 – 500 (Slightly Creepy Scary)
      501 – 750 (Alone-in-the-Dark Scary)
      751 – 1000 (Knee-Shaking, Heart-Pounding, Halloween-at-
                  Midnight Scary)

NOW HIRING!

New jobs are always opening up at HorrorLand—but we need these special assignments filled fast!

HOUSECREEPING ASSISTANT
Stagger Inn's only had one housecreeper—the thirteen-foot-tall Linda—since it opened. But now that Linda's getting a little older (she just turned 402), she needs an assistant to help her with some of the more physical chores, like shaking spiders out of the sheets and pouring garbage out of the windows.

DANCING SQUIDS STAGE MOPPER
It might sound easy, but mopping up after a squid show is actually one of the toughest, slipperiest jobs in HorrorLand because of the huge amounts of slime squids make when they dance. Don't apply unless you have good balance, a strong back, and don't mind the smell of seafood.

A-NILE-ATOR REPAIR PERSON

The lines are always long for HorrorLand's scariest, most popular ride. And because it's always busy, the A-Nile-Ator is always in need of repair. We're looking for someone who knows how to use tape, chewing gum, and string to make quick roller coaster fixes—so we can keep the lines moving.

QUICKSAND BEACH LIFEGUARD

No swimming skills needed. Quicksand Beach lifeguards only have two responsibilities: warning guests not to go in the water and filling out the "missing person" forms when they do.

HIGH-SKILL JOBS

Some of the jobs in HorrorLand require more than a pair of horns and a spiny tail—they require special training, previous on-the-job experience, or even a special degree.

ROBOT REPAIR TECHNICIAN

For security reasons, we can't tell you what kind of robots we're talking about until after you're hired—but we can say that there's a LOT more going on behind the scenes at HorrorLand than most humans think. We're looking for a monster with these qualifications:

- A history of taking apart household appliances for no good reason
- Experience dealing with cranky, overworked electronic devices
- Someone who's strong enough to wrestle misbehaving robots to the ground

Applicants should be comfortable with working long hours underground and OK with getting frequent electric shocks.

THEY MUST BE TALKING ABOUT THE ROBOTS IN THE TUNNELS UNDER THE PARK!
— LM1

LABORATORY ASSISTANT

Again, we're not at liberty to say exactly what TYPE of lab or experiments we're talking about—but rest assured, HorrorLand's scientists are on the biting edge of monster-related genetic research. We're looking for someone to help those scientists with everyday tasks like:

• Cleaning weird blue gooey stuff out of the bottoms of cages
• Reading bedtime stories to weird-looking creatures
• Providing first aid to injured scientists

Experience fighting gorillas is a plus.

WEREWOLF FUR STYLIST

You wouldn't believe how fussy werewolves can be about their appearance—that's why HorrorLand keeps a full-time staff of stylists on hand to wash, trim, blow dry, and style the fur of our villagers. Experienced hairstylists are needed for:

• Weekly snout trims and underarm shampoos
• Fancy tail puffs, braids, and ear fur highlights
• Claw clipping and polishing

• MONSTERS OF THE MONTH •

Every month we celebrate two employees who represent the best
of what HorrorLand has to offer. Each recipient gets a framed
certificate and five extra pounds of their preferred monthly salary.

SERGEANT CLEM MUNCIE:
HEAD OF THE MONSTER POLICE

At one point or another, every monster that works in HorrorLand
will see Sergeant Clem chasing after a misbehaving guest – growling,
threatening, and gnashing his fangs. It's what he's always done best.
"I've been an MP since the park first opened," he says, "and I still
get a thrill every time I get to make a human miserable." As a young
member of the Monster Police, Clem was so enthusiastic that he
actually designed the MPs' black-and-orange uniforms himself. We
salute him for keeping the park safe and the humans scared.

Security Level: 5 (Entire park)
Preferred Salary: Live maggots
Employee Since: Day 1

MORGANA: MASK MAKER

Morgana's only been at the park for a few months, but she's already
become a familiar face – actually a LOT of familiar faces. She's
the assistant mask maker at Zombie Plaza's new store, MAKE A
FACE, where she creates masks that are so lifelike, some guests are
convinced they're real. When we asked her what her secret was, she
said, "When I see someone with a face I like, I'll do whatever it takes
to add it to my permanent collection. That's all I can say."
Keep up the good work, Morgana!

Security Level: 2 (Zombie Plaza only)
Preferred Salary: Toenail clippings
Employee Since: Less than one year

MEMO TO EMPLOYEES: THE WRONG KIND OF MONSTER

TO: All HorrorLand Employees
FROM: Les Chompem
Director of Monster Resources
RE: The Horror known as "Byron"

Dear Employees,

I'm sad to report that some disturbing news has come to my attention. While most HorrorLand employees are committed to scaring humans, lying to them, and making them as uncomfortable as possible—it seems that one of our trusted Horrors, Byron, has dishonestly, despicably, and disgustingly betrayed HorrorLand by HELPING some of its human guests.

We have proof that Byron has shared classified information with young humans, given them key cards, and left them clues about some of HorrorLand's most closely guarded secrets.

I should've seen this coming—after all, everyone knows that you can't trust a monster with blue eyes. We haven't decided what Byron's punishment will be (but our friends in the Monster Police have offered a long list of suggestions).

Let this be a lesson to all of us . . .

It only takes one good apple to spoil the bunch.

Les Chompem
Director of Monster Resources

PARK UPKEEP & IMPROVEMENTS

ESCAPE
www.EnterHorrorLand.com

GUEST BINDER
SECTION 8:

PARK UPKEEP & IMPROVEMENTS

Message from Doug Hisgrave
Vice President of Park Operations

Keeping HorrorLand running takes a monstrous behind-the-scenes effort. There are always rides that need repairs, creatures that need feeding, accidents that need to be covered up, and new attractions that need to be installed (usually after the old ones unexpectedly collapse). It's my job to make sure that hundreds of Horrors, vampires, werewolves, shopkeepers, innkeepers, and bat keepers work together to keep the park running smoother than a squid's eyelids. Every day, my staff and I write memos, read employee suggestions, and dream up new ways to make HorrorLand THE MOST TERRIFYING PLACE ON EARTH.

On an average day, the Park Operations Office (POO) releases anywhere from 1 to 57 memos with urgent updates for HorrorLand employees. In an effort to assure all our guests of our total commitment to their (or our) enjoyment, allow us to share some of the recent updates.

MEMO

To: All Crude Cart Staff
From: Mr. Pew K. Latte
Re: Crude Cart Guidelines

It has been brought to my attention that some Crude Cart workers are not following the HorrorLand FDA* Requirements.

Please review the following guidelines to keep your carts unclean, unsafe, and unhealthy:

- **Accept delivery from Ripe Garb Age Service every morning.**

- **Kids will be demanding extra larvae and extra maggots. Keep a good supply.**

- **If you sneeze on the food you are selling, do not wipe it off with your hand; please recycle a used tissue (HorrorLand is always thinking Green).**

If you have any questions, please direct them to yourself.

*Foul and Disgusting Administration

MEMO

To: All HorrorLand Staff
From: Doug Hisgrave
Re: Park Procedures

Effective immediately, the following changes have been made to HorrorLand's operating guidelines:

TREATMENT OF GUESTS

We appreciate the extra mile some of you go to scare our human guests, but due to an avalanche of complaints and lawsuits, Horrors are no longer allowed to:

• Lock guests in the Vampire State Building overnight. (The vampires were complaining they couldn't get any sleep!)

• Point guests to Wolfsbane Forest when they ask for directions to the exit—remember, we don't want the werewolves to gain too much weight.

• Loosen seat belts on the A-Nile-Ator.

• Replace the heads in the Guillotine Museum even though the old ones are getting pretty wrinkled.

EXITING THE PARK

Every guest must receive a hand stamp when exiting the park – no exceptions. For most guests, this means getting a little purple skull stamped on the backs of their hands. But for our Very Special Guests, it means the purple "H" stamp. If they resist or start asking questions, mumble something about a big prize giveaway and stamp their hands before they have a chance to stop you.

DRESS CODE

Many monsters (myself included) find clothing to be weird and uncomfortable – but since HorrorLand depends on human guests, we have to respect their customs. Up till now, we've made exceptions for werewolves and other furry monsters. But due to new regulations, all Horrors are now required to wear ties . . . just ties.

Thank you for your attention in these matters.

MEMO

To: All Park Staff
From: Sergeant Clem Muncie
Re: Park Security

As a reminder to all park employees, the following items are forbidden in HorrorLand:

Cameras

(Flashes can hurt the eyes of our park creatures — at least, that's what we tell guests.)

Cell phones and laptops with Internet

(The "official" reason is that their signals interfere with park safety equipment. But I think we all know the real reason.)

Mirrors

(Again, the "official" reason is that broken glass could hurt guests.)

Any guest found with these items should be taken to Monster Police headquarters immediately.

YEAH, BUT THE REAL REASON THEY DON'T WANT MIRRORS IN HORRORLAND IS BECAUSE OF PANIC PARK! —LM1

EMPLOYEE SUGGESTION BOX

The Park Operations Office has a box where any employee can offer his/her/its suggestion for improvements to HorrorLand. And since we really want to know what you think, we've placed it in an alligator cage in the middle of the Landmine Maze. So drop us a note (if you dare), and we'll do our best to get back to you in the next five to seven years. Here are some examples of employee suggestions (and our responses):

Suggestion

Your Name: Phil Koffens

Your Job: Park Doctor

Your Suggestion: How do you expect me to treat people when you won't even pay for basic medical supplies?

Our Response: We don't.

Suggestion

Your Name: T. Rona Sorus

Your Job: Cashier, Stagger Inn Gift Chop

Your Suggestion: I'd like to file a complaint against my coworker Cindy. She treats me like she's my boss or something!

Our Response: We checked, Rona. Cindy *is* your boss.

Suggestion

Your Name: Hugh Bluitt

Your Job: Monster Police Officer

Your Suggestion: Can we have a day off to be with our families on Halloween?

Our Response: You can have as many days as you want, Hugh. You're fired.

Suggestion

Your Name: Wally Waits

Your Job: Lab Assistant

Your Suggestion: We need newer, stronger cages for those blue-eyed gorilla things we're working on down here. They're so easy to open, a child could figure it out! Actually, a child did figure it out!

Our Response: Shhh! No one's supposed to know about those!

Suggestion

Your Name: Jenny Furr

Your Job: Werewolf

Your Suggestion: No suggestion . . . I just wanted to say that I really love working here!

Our Response: Nobody likes a kiss-up, Jenny. You're fired.

P.O.P. QUIZ
(PARK OPERATIONS PREPAREDNESS)

From time to time, the Park Operations Office gives surprise P.O.P. quizzes to random employees. They're designed to see if you know how to handle the many situations that might come up in HorrorLand. A good grade could mean a promotion – and a bad grade could mean, well . . . you're fired. We've provided some questions from an older quiz below. Study hard – you never know when it's your turn to P.O.P.!

Werewolves are keeping guests awake by howling at the moon. Do you:
- A – Threaten to report them to the Monster Police?
- B – Politely ask them to keep the noise down?
- C – Put muzzles over their snouts?
- D – Let them howl, since they'll probably eat you if you try A, B, or C?

There are too many worms in the Tunnel of Screams. Do you:
- A – Start eating worms as fast as you can?
- B – Trick question – there can never be too many worms in the Tunnel of Screams!
- C – Donate the extra worms to the nearest restaurant?
- D – Politely ask some of the worms to leave?

One of the bolts on the Scary-Go-Round is dangerously loose. Do you:
- A – Replace it with a new bolt?
- B – Put some chewing gum on it and hope it holds?
- C – Make the ride spin even faster?
- D – Start running in circles, screaming and waving your arms like crazy?

Answers: D, B, C (we would have also accepted D)

The Silver Bulletin

HORRORLAND ANNOUNCES
"Give Us Your Worst!"
CONTEST FOR EMPLOYEES!

by Wolf Blister

For the first time in park history, the Park Operations Office is inviting employees to come up with HorrorLand's next big attraction. "We're looking for a great idea," said Doug Hisgrave, VP of Park Operations, "and we don't care if it comes from a vampire or a bellboy at Stagger Inn." Mr. Hisgrave said he's open to ideas for new rides, new stage shows, new restaurants – even new ways of cleaning up bat droppings. He'll pick the three best ideas, and HorrorLand employees will vote for the winner. The first-place finisher will get to see his/her/its idea come to life and receive his/her/its choice of 1,000 pounds of maggots, toenail clippings, or squid slime. Second place will receive a year's supply of Gassy Hippo perfume, and third place will receive a copy of "Tunnel of Screams' Greatest Screams" on CD. The contest is open to all employees. Ideas must be submitted in writing to the Park Operations Office by midnight tomorrow.

WEREWOLVES PROTEST NEW "CLOTHING" RULE
by Harry Knight, Cub Reporter

WEREWOLF VILLAGE— Dozens of werewolves gathered in the village center today to protest the new HorrorLand rule requiring all employees to wear clothing. Some held signs with slogans like "Wear Pants? Not a Chance!" Others tore shirts and socks apart with their teeth. It was the latest in a series of unusual behavior by these furry beasts. Something has got them riled and we're determined to find out what.

V.I.V.'s:

VERY IMPORTANT VILLAINS

ESCAPE
www.EnterHorrorLand.com

GUEST BINDER
SECTION 9:

V.I.V.'s:
VERY IMPORTANT VILLAINS

HorrorLand has always been a popular destination for the evil elite.
Whenever a V.I.V. (Very Important Villain) visits, it's my job to make sure
they have an absolutely miserable stay, from custom sleeping coffins
to special hard-to-catch meals. But I can't do it alone. As HorrorLand
employees, we should be able to spot Very Important Villains and cater
to their demands, threats, and temper tantrums quickly and effectively.
So please read this section closely, and remember — together, we can
all make sure our V.I.V.'s receive the worst care possible.

Di Kwickley
Viceroy of Guest Relations

V.I.V.'s: VERY IMPORTANT VILLAINS

We're so proud of all the terrible clientele we've attracted over the years, especially the villains who have that little bit of extra evil. These individuals represent the very best of HorrorLand's worst guests:

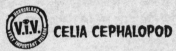 CELIA CEPHALOPOD

Originally one of HorrorLand's dancing squids, Celia quit the stage to devote herself to attacking sea vessels full time.

Amazing Accomplishment: Single-handedly sank a cruise ship even though one of her tentacles was sprained
Fascinating Fact: Cries when she watches *Titanic* (feels sorry for the iceberg)
Quintessential Quote: "No ship can escape my grip!"

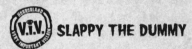 SLAPPY THE DUMMY

Don't let his name fool you – Slappy is one of the *smartest*, meanest villains ever to set tiny wooden feet in HorrorLand!

Amazing Accomplishment: Survived having a moldy sandwich stuffed in his head
Fascinating Fact: Carved from coffin wood
Quintessential Quote: "Is that your face, or did your neck throw up?"

BRADLEY D. KADE

A mummy who can gain control of anyone's mind just by looking into her eyes; makes his victims do gross or embarrassing things for his amusement.

Amazing Accomplishment: Once made a school bus full of kids eat their own boogers for ten hours straight

Fascinating Fact: Has his bandages custom made in Italy

Quintessential Quote: "Want to have a staring contest?"

 ## DREW QUARTZ

A vampire pop superstar whose album *Coffin Sneeze* went to #1 on the Billblood charts.

Amazing Accomplishment: Sold out HorrorLand's Haunted Theater twenty nights in a row

Fascinating Fact: Had his fangs whitened by a dentist

Quintessential Quote: "Oh, girl, it's much too bright — I can only go to the beach at night." (from the song "Beach at Night")

 ## DR. MANIAC

A supervillain with a flair for fashion and a mind for mayhem — so evil and powerful that he escaped from the Internet to wreak real-world havoc.

Amazing Accomplishment: Kidnapped a whole town full of kids

Fascinating Fact: Enjoys eating dead squirrels

Quintessential Quote: "I'm not crazy...I'm a MANIAC!"

SNARLA SNOUTENHEIM

Snarla grew up in HorrorLand's own Werewolf Village but ran away
after being teased by humans. As the founder of the Four-Footed
Freedom Fighters, she's vowed to turn every single human into
a werewolf.

Amazing Accomplishment: Set the world record for "Most Humans
Bitten in One Night" (541)

Fascinating Fact: Was born Fluffles Furrykins but changed
her name to Snarla Snoutenheim to sound
meaner

Quintessential Quote: "No snout? No fur? You're OUT! Yessir!"

 ## SIRIUS HUNCH

The headless human hunter who's never failed to find his man (or
woman, or kid), even though he doesn't have any eyes, ears, or brains.

Amazing Accomplishment: Once tracked a group of kids through five
miles of woods by feeling the ground with
his hands

Fascinating Fact: Loves neckties, even though he doesn't have
a neck

Quintessential Quote: (No quotes available - doesn't have a mouth)

V.I.V. SUPERSTARS

All of our V.I.V.'s deserve special treatment, but when these three show up in HorrorLand, we *really* roll out the black carpet. They're our top three villain superstars:

DREW QUARTZ

There's no question about it — Drew is the world's most famous undead singing sensation. He may look like a regular music star, but that handsome young face (he's barely over 100 years old — *super* young for a vampire) hides an ugly, evil heart. His music has the power to hypnotize people who listen to it, making them easy targets for thirsty vampires. When he's not recording a new song in his home dungeon or going to the hottest nightclubs in Transylvania, he's thinking up new ways to turn his fans into food.

VILLAINOMETER:

DR. MANIAC

Dr. Maniac, a.k.a. The Totally Mental Maniac of Mayhem, didn't *choose* to be evil and insane —a boy named Robby Schwartz *created* him that way. His leopard cape and yellow-feathered boots are just as crazy as his warped mind — and since he can jump in and out of TV and computer screens, Dr. Maniac can pop up and cause trouble *anywhere* at *anytime*. When he's visiting HorrorLand (and he isn't making things freeze, fly, or blow up), you'll probably find him shopping for colorful tights in Zombie Plaza.

VILLAINOMETER:

SLAPPY THE DUMMY

Slappy is the one villain who makes other villains tremble with fear. Yes, he's small. Yes, he's made of wood. Yes, he wears a bow tie – but his nasty insults have the power to ruin *anyone's* day. There's no V.I.V. who has more power to hurt feelings, and no V.I.V. who makes more demands when he stays at HorrorLand. "I admit it," says Slappy, "I'm a control freak. I need things a certain way, or I get cranky. And when I get cranky, bad things happen." HorrorLand will do anything to keep Slappy happy – including closing rides so he can have them all to himself. (Once, Slappy rode the R.I.P.P.E.R. DIPPER for two days straight.)

VILLAINOMETER:

MEMO

TO: All Stagger Inn Staff
FROM: Pearl E. Gates, Innkeeper
RE: Special Needs of V.I.V. Guests

We have an unusually high number of Very Important Villains staying
with us this week, and each of them has his or her own special
demands. Please review and make sure each one is carried out
(otherwise, you'll be carried out):

· Slappy the Dummy demands that we check his room for termites
  twice a day. He also wants an extra sprinkler system installed in his
  room in case there's a fire.

· Sirius Hunch wants all the pillows removed from his room. Pillows
  remind him that he doesn't have a head . . . and that makes him sad.

· Dr. Maniac would like a walk-in closet built for his feathered-boot
  collection. He would like this closet to be made of marshmallows.
  Why? Because he's a *maniac*.

· Celia Cephalopod wants an extra-large bathtub placed where the bed
  usually goes. She'd also like several toy boats placed in the tub so she
  can practice sinking them.

· Drew Quartz has specifically requested silk coffin sheets and a 9 pm
  wake-up call.

As always, if you have questions, please direct them to yourself.

Pearl E. Gates

HOW TO LOOK LIKE A V.I.V.

Just because you aren't a Very Important Villain doesn't mean you can't *look* like one. Here are a few ways to achieve that V.I.V. style without breaking the bank:

★ CLOTHING ★

All the top villains are wearing authentic "zombie" clothes this year – but why pay more when you can get that same style for pennies? Just take any old clothes, rip some holes in them, rub them in dirt, and presto – you look like a zombie!

★★ HAIR CARE ★★

V.I.V.'s prefer Dead Head Sculpting Mousse ("Guaranteed to be the *last* hair product you ever buy!"). But one ounce costs more than most Horrors make in a month. To achieve the same stylish look for less, simply rub a handful of snot on your fur and let it harden.

★ JEWELRY ★

One of the hottest V.I.V. jewelry items is a bat-fang necklace – but they can "suck" the money right out of your wallet. Instead, try pulling out all of your *own* teeth, tying them to a string, and wearing them around your neck. Also saves you a lifetime of money on toothpaste!

★★ ACCESSORIES ★★

Alligator bags (bags made from real *living* alligators) can cost an arm and a leg (literally) at department stores like Gloomindale's. To get that "snappy" look for less, try catching a large lizard and training it to be a purse.

STAGGER INN
GUESTBOOK

I LOVE Stagger Inn — except for
all the HUMANS staying here!
— Snarla Snoutenheim

FANGS FOR THE FREE ROOM
— DREW

STAGGER INN IS HEAD AND SHOULDERS
ABOVE THE REST! — Sirius Hench

SEE you NEXt tiME, SLAVES!
— SLAPPY tHE DUMMY

Hate to "wrap" up my stay,
but I've got to go visit
MY MUMMY! — Bradley D. Kade

The Silver Bulletin

NEWS & GOSSIP

PURPLE RAGE & DR. MANIAC BFF's?

Everyone knows that purple and yellow look good together – but we never thought we'd live to see the day that the Purple Rage and the yellow-feather-booted Dr. Maniac would be spotted smiling and shaking hands! That's exactly what one of our tipsters witnessed yesterday in Good-bye Land. Does this mean their long-running feud is over? Or will they be battling again before we can say . . . **VILLAINS AND HUMANS WORKING TOGETHER?** Are certain V.I.V.'s joining forces with some of HorrorLand's human guests? We know it sounds impossible, but rumors of a Top Secret Project are making their way around the park. Details are sketchy, but our spies are on the case.

THE
POWER
OF 10

GUEST BINDER
SECTION 10:

THE POWER OF 10

Way back during the park's 10th Anniversary Year, attendance started to die off (and that's the ONE thing we DON'T want to die off in HorrorLand!). People were getting bored with the same old rides and the same old shops. I warned everybody that if we couldn't bring any new customers in (and fast), we'd have to close the park forever. Can you imagine? Where would the werewolves go? What would happen to the creatures in Loch Ness Lake? Do you know how hard it is for our Horrors to find jobs in the "normal" world? They're too ugly to work anywhere else! Lucky for them, I'm a genius and came up with a plan to give HorrorLand a makeover!

The Ten Haunted Acres

The first thing we did was buy the ten-acre haunted cemetery next to the park and start building on it. Rather than throw away all those tombstones, we used them to build all sorts of things that you can still see today: ticket counters, tables at the Pretzel Pal, and steps leading up to the R.I.P.P.E.R. Dipper, to name a few. Because of this, Monster Police deal with a heavy number of angry ghosts in the area, especially since we started moving coffins to Good-Bye Land. But the coolest thing we built on this new cemetery land was the tallest, grossest, scariest ride in the entire park (and also the greatest publicity stunt in HorrorLand's history).

The Rise of the Doom Slide

The same day that HorrorLand started building in the cemetery, we also announced a planet-wide contest to design the park's newest, wildest ride: THE DOOM SLIDE. Just about every single living ride designer on earth (and a few un-living ones) submitted their fastest, gloopiest, and most dangerous blueprints. Instead of picking one winner, HorrorLand picked ten random designs and combined them into one ride. What they ended up with was the giant purple mayhem-maker that we now know and fear today: THE DOOM SLIDE — with ten terrifying ways to slide to your screaming doom.

We tested each of the ten slides over and over until our test riders were all out of barf, and our safety inspectors were sure that there was NOTHING safe about the new ride. No part of the slides went untouched by Horror hurl. But when opening day came, something weird happened . . . the riders began to disappear. People who screamed their way down the Doom Slide never reached the bottom. That first day, the line for the Doom Slide stretched ten miles, with an estimated wait time of ten days.

The park was saved.

Bill Board
Head of HorrorLand Advertising

THE DOOM SLIDE:
10 WAYS TO MEET YOUR DOOM

Below is a "slide-by-slide" comparison of the Doom Slide's ten different routes. There's no height requirement, and your only safety bar is a boa constrictor.

#1 – EAR WAX ALLEY

Did you know that ear wax is an excellent slide wax, too? This awful-tasting dive is one of the ride's fastest (but you can't hear a thing for 10 weeks after riding it!).

#2 – THE ELECTRIC BANSHEE

What's more shocking? Howling banshees chasing you or 10 electric shocks at every bend? Why choose?!? This plunge has them both!

#3 – THE WORM BELLY

Riders experience every slime-drenched detail of being digested in the intestines of a giant 200-foot worm. The slowest of the slides, it takes ten years to complete. (You only travel 20 feet a year!)

#4 – DRAGONBREATH DIVE

A dark, breakneck race over a series of pitch-black loops. This one's surprisingly survivable — unless you happen to slide down during one of the random "Dragonbreath" blasts, when the entire slide fills up with 1,000-degree green-and-purple fire. But hey — at least you'll be able to see!

#5 – THE JUST-A-DROP

Should this even be considered a slide? The drop is not just steep. It's straight down. Isn't this just buying a ticket to jump off a cliff? You bet! What a thrill!

#6 - THE HAIRY LUGE

Ten bristling loops down a slide covered in greasy, slippery, damp hair. It's not alive (right?), but it could use some serious shampoo.

#7 - THE CARPENTER'S DELIGHT

Filled with twists and loops, and lined with miles of sandpaper, nails, and saw blades!

#8 - THE SEWER SLIDE

This slide doubles as the main artery for HorrorLand's waste-control system. It's smellier on hot days, wetter and more clogged up on busy days, and very, very dangerous on alligator days.

#9 - THE INFINITY DREADFUL

Endless. Forever sliding to nowhere. We're not even quite sure how we know. It's just that no one has ever come out the bottom . . . not that we even know where the bottom is. Definitely pack a hearty lunch.

#10 - SO THAT'S WHERE ALL THE AXES WENT!

When the Slide was under construction, many Horrors started to notice their axes were going missing. Stagger Inn's were stolen. The Woodsmen of Wolfsbane Forest were weaponless. The answer was revealed on Doom Slide Day! Here they all are! Swinging right at your head while you're sliding at 100 miles an hour! Mystery solved! Duck!

IMPOSTER ALERT!
INTRUDER ALERT!

The slippery spy is still on the loose here in HorrorLand.
Should you nab the evildoer, here are more questions to see if
he needs to visit The Keeper . . . permanently.

The Monster Police are to be:
- A. Avoided.
- B. Obeyed.
- C. Honored in song and poetry.
- D. Right behind you at all times.

The show currently playing at the Haunted Theater is:
- A. Guys and Skulls.
- B. Mondo the Magical.
- C. Jersey Devils.
- D. Bats! The Musical.

Housecreeper Linda's shoe size is:
- A. Impossible to measure.
- B. Linda doesn't wear shoes.
- C. Nobody's ever had the courage to ask her.
- D. 26.

Madame Doom's fortunes:
- A. Always come true.
- B. Always rhyme.
- C. Make me sleepy.
- D. Should not be trusted under any circumstances.

The Pretzel Pal stand offers all seasonings except:

    A. Rat-tooth sprinkles.

    B. Snot-cho cheese.

    C. Dingo drool.

    D. Mustard. (Ew! That would be so gross!)

The Robot Guards at the Good-Bye Land gate:

    A. Are just there to protect you.

    B. Totally don't have hidden cameras in their eyes.

    C. Certainly can't come to life.

    D. All of the above

Reading another person's mind is:

    A. Forbidden on HorrorLand grounds.

    B. Not actually possible.

    C. A nifty way to ace a pop quiz.

    D. An excellent way for us to find the spy!

GULP! DON'T LET THEM FIND YOU!
BONE UP ON YOUR FACTS AT
WWW.ESCAPEHORRORLAND.COM
—LIZZY

TOP SECRET
DOCUMENT

FAMOUS BURIALS IN
GOOD-BYE LAND

Some people think that Good-Bye Land Cemetery holds
the bodies of everyone who's ever died in HorrorLand.
That's crazy! It's WAY too small! But it DOES contain the
bones of some of the weirdest, coolest individuals who've
had the pleasure to perish here.

Here are the 10 most interesting interred inside:

WYATT BURP

The famous gunfighter with a throaty belch and an unnatural
love for sarsaparilla died here after downing the jug of Monster
Blood he'd snuck in.

HORROR O'HORROHAN

Former Chief of Monster Police, buried in his Orange & Blacks with a
Coffin Cake in his hand (and some evidence that needed hiding).

GUS ZOONTIGHT

Being a werewolf allergic to animal fur is nothing to sneeze at.

THE TOMB OF UNKNOWN GARDENERS

This crypt contains the remains of all the HorrorLand gardeners
who've ignored our warnings about the Man-Eating Plant.

REGINALD, THE DEAD ROBOT

A medical miracle. Before Reggie kicked the bucket of bolts,
we didn't even know it was possible for robots to die.

FRYRA BANKS

This famous model was here to promote her new line of hairspray and
got WAY too close to Stagger Inn's fire-breathing hair dryers.

THE CHICKEN THAT CROSSED THE ROAD

The VERY bird that inspired the age-old joke was squashed on his
way across HorrorLand Drive (by a truck delivering our daily
quicksand supply). Some suspect fowl play.

ANYA TOES

No more ballet in the Haunted Theater. The theater doesn't like it.

BARBIE Q. MISHAP

When Barbie was hired to work in the HorrorLand cafeteria, she
used fresh, un-maggot-ridden hamburger meat!
(So the Horrors buried her in it.)

HALF OF PETE

Luckily, it was the half with the name tag.

NOW OPENING:
THE BRAIN STAND!!!

Thanks to generous donations by the ten geniuses who've died at HorrorLand over the years, our own HorrorLand Witch Doctor—erm—*Brain* Doctor: Dr. Sarah Bellum Ph.D. Esq. Vi.V., finally has all of the raw materials she needs to unveil our newest attraction: THE BRAIN STAND!

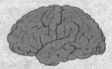

Dr. Bellum Ph.D. Esq. Vi.V. promises that the Brain Stand is a more intelligent undertaking than all the other kiosks that have failed on the same spot. (Who can forget how quickly the Heart Stand was attacked by critics? Many found the Toe Stand too cheesy. And no one could believe the gall of the Bladder Stand.)

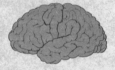

So what can you do at the Brain Stand? GROW YOUR OWN MIND POWERS! We strap you to the stand's pulsing Brain Shell with high-powered electrodes, free of charge. Though we must warn you that there is one slight side effect associated with whichever Mind Power you choose. So strap in and take your pick!

MIND POWER #1: Pass any test you ever take for the rest of your life.

       Side Effect: You can't see the color red or anything with polka dots.

MIND POWER #2: Make any taste happen in your mouth whenever you want it.

       Side Effect: No sense of direction. Always lost. Even when at home.

MIND POWER #3: You can play video games without touching the controller.

       Side Effect: Everything looks like it is plaid and has a plaid cabbage on top of it.

MIND POWER #4: You can read any book in six seconds.

       Side Effect: You always feel like you have three different paper cuts.

MIND POWER #5: You can talk to all animals except pigeons.

       Side Effect: You always think someone is tapping you on the left shoulder.

MIND POWER #6: You only need to sleep for one minute every day.
    Side Effect: Everything will always taste like pickle juice . . . except pickles.

MIND POWER #7: You remember everybody's name. Even if you've never met them.
    Side Effect: You forget second grade . . . forever.

MIND POWER #8: No one can ever tell that you're lying or keeping a secret.
    Side Effect: You can only sleep outside and with one shoe on.

MIND POWER #9: You can make up the best stories the world has ever heard.
    Side Effect: Every time you try to say "yes," you say "rutabaga juice" instead.

MIND POWER #10: We take your brain out and put it in a jar for you to look at!
    Side Effect: We've taken out your brain! And it's in a jar!

VAMPIRE VILLAGE

VAMPIRE VILLAGE

A Bloody Good Time

It used to be easy to be undead . . . but with so many movies and books painting vampires in a bad light (actually, when you're a vampire, ALL light is bad light) and new vampire-hunting technologies like GPS (Garlic-Poisoned Stakes), it's getting pretty tough out there for us vamps. That's why we asked HorrorLand to build Vampire Village—so bloodsuckers could have a place to hang their capes, bury their coffins, and feel at home. A place where they could party all night and sleep all day, far away from the reach of those outrageous sun-loving humans.

Countess Shirley Thirsty
Vampire Village Living & Undead Relations

FAQs – Freakishly Absurd Questions About The Vampire State Building

This jet-black and bloodred skyscraper is the tallest structure ever built by Horrors. An architect once planned to top it by building The Fears Tower, but he "mysteriously" fell to his demise researching the Vampire State's observation deck. (Two things every architect should know: 1. Vampires don't use railings. 2. Vampires don't like people building taller skyscrapers than theirs.)

Q: What are the biggest businesses in the Vampire State Building?

A: All of the major vampire magazines are published here. And it's also the home of the Transylvanian Embassy. But the biggest business of all is the vampires themselves. They outgrew the Village long ago and now, during daylight hours, the VSB is a massive vampire hotel.

Q: How many vampires live in the Vampire State Building?

A: Vampires don't like to be called "living." And the number of vamps that call the VSB home is far too vast to Count. Plus, the population keeps getting higher as more HorrorLand guests pay it a visit, so, who knows? Maybe you'll be its next resident!

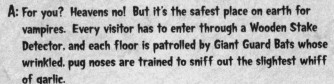

Q: Is it safe?

A: For you? Heavens no! But it's the safest place on earth for vampires. Every visitor has to enter through a Wooden Stake Detector, and each floor is patrolled by Giant Guard Bats whose wrinkled, pug noses are trained to sniff out the slightest whiff of garlic.

FAQs – Freakishly Absurd Questions About The Vampire State Building

Q: Is this the only skyscraper that wears a cape?

A: Yes.

Q: Why aren't there any stairs?

A: Vampires don't tend to use them. You may be able to hitch a ride from one of the residents in his bat form. If not, the Vampire State Building's coffin-sized elevators are a snug but scary ride (for one) all the way to the top. (Bring a crowbar with you . . . we're not exactly sure who lets you out at the top.)

Q: Why doesn't Count Dracula live here?

A: He prefers to stay at the Stagger Inn. When he invites its other guests up to his room "for a drink," they aren't quite as suspecting of what he means.

FAQs – Freakishly Absurd Questions About The Vampire State Building

Located in Vampire Village at the intersection of Hollywood & Vein, The Vampire State Building is the tallest structure in HorrorLand.

Q: How Can I Find the Vampire State Building?

A: Follow the Yellow Guano Road. Don't try asking any vampires for directions— they can be a pain in the neck!

Q: What's inside?

A: PLASMA PLAZA –shops like Fangs for the Memories Antiques and restaurants like Dracula's Stake House. The upper floors have BAT-ting cages and a 6-scream movie theater with all-coffin seating.

Q: Can I go to the top?

A: Yes! Our observation deck is open every night from sundown to sunrise and offers a one-of-a-kind view of HorrorLand. All we ask is a small donation from each guest (one or two pints, depending on your size).

Q: Why are all the windows blacked out?

A: Please hurry over so we can answer that question for you in person!

FRIGHTSEEING VAMPIRE VILLAGE WITH
SICK STEVES

Sniffle. Burp. Yuk . . . what am I writing again? Oh, yeah. Hi! *Belch.* I'm Sick Steves and I'm—*cough*—I'm here to tell you how to see all the frights of Vampire Village fast—*sneezesniffle*—and on any budget— *burp*—sorry, I'm not feeling so good.

🦇 *VAMPIRE VILLAGE IN A FLASH* 🦇

Many guests—*hiccup*—understandably want to see all of the frights of Vampire Village in one day . . . so they can be safely home before the sun sets. Here are some quick tips to ensure that you don't stay past your host's wake-up time:

DON'T TALK TO BLOWHARD BARTHOLOMEW
The Worm & Bait Shop cashier has never told a story shorter than nine hours long. And they're all about worms.

SKIP THE BAT BARN
By the end of the day, you'll have seen plenty, believe me. Why take the time to see a bunch more, all in tiny stables? *Barf.*

RUN!
There are Countless reasons why this is wise advice that saves far more than just time. Wear good comfortable sneakers or roller skates.

🦇 *VAMPIRE VILLAGE ON A DIME* 🦇

No money? Gak. Not a problem. Shops and vendors here take all "types" of currency. Nevertheless, here are some tips to keep them from bleeding you dry:

BRING YOUR OWN LUNCH
The residents here have no use for snack bars. Do not picnic on Vulture Beach, however, unless you want to be the main course.

CRUISE CONTROL
See the wonders of The Mind Swamp from shore and skip the expensive and (six times out of five) deadly Coffin Cruise. *Aah-choo!*

DON'T TAKE THE BAIT
Before buying "fancy" worms at The Worm & Bait Shop, ask yourself, "Do these worms really taste better than the worms I have at home?"

🦇 *VAMPIRE VILLAGE FOR BIRD-WATCHERS* 🦇
There are an amazing variety of birds in Vampire Village. Ornithologists from around the world perch here to spy on the dazzling array of black vultures, Egyptian vultures, vampire vultures—cough (okay, so there're only vultures). Sometimes, if you're lucky, you can see a pretty blue jay or a robin fly into the Village . . . and then get eaten by one of the vultures.

🦇 *VAMPIRE VILLAGE FOR* 🦇 *FLYING MAMMAL-WATCHERS*
Batter up! The only time you can't see the bats is when there are so many above you that they blot out the sun. This only tends to happen between breakfast and dinner.

VAMPIRE VILLAGE BUSINESS CARDS

Vampires stay up late. In fact, that's the only time they stay up.
These businesses are open from sunset to sunrise to accommodate
their dark, vampiric rush hours.

CARCASSES "R" US
WHEN IT ABSOLUTELY, POSITIVELY,
BETTER NOT BE FRESH MEAT!

WHERE DO YOU THINK THEY GET ALL THE DEAD MEAT FROM?

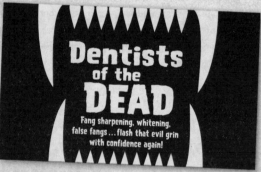

Dentists of the DEAD
Fang sharpening, whitening,
false fangs...flash that evil grin
with confidence again!

SHARPENING?!?
AREN'T THEY ALREADY
SHARP ENOUGH?!?

SPECIALIZING IN THE HEALTHCARE NEEDS
OF THE IMMORTAL AND UNDEAD.

WHY WOULD A VAMPIRE NEED HEALTH INSURANCE?

HORROR HANDYMAN/HELPER

"I'm always there when ya need me. Trust me."

HE'S ON OUR SIDE... RIGHT?

CRUISIN' THE MIND SWAMP ...
IN A COFFIN!

We know ... it sounds too perfect, doesn't it?!? Too romantic. Too swampy. But let us assure you that swampy romance exists—and we're ready to set sail! Here's just a taste of what we promise:

BEAUTIFULLY DETAILED COFFIN BOATS

Every ship is individually carved and painted with its own gory artwork—each depicts a famous vampire or vulture attack. Though originally built with just one "passenger" in mind, we've sometimes stuffed as many as seven guests into one coffin! What fun!

EXCITING MIND SWAMP "BRAIN-WATCHING"

Keep your eyes peeled for gooey, dripping brains bobbing in the bubbling swamp. A true natural mystery!

NO LIFE PRESERVERS

Sooo bulky and uncomfortable. Who needs the hassle?

GUARANTEED TO SINK!

Who else can make that promise? We've learned over time that just because something is made out of wood doesn't mean it will float. See The Mind Swamp from its most beautiful spot—the bottom!

So come on down! This body of water could use some more bodies!

Capt. Vlad the Smooth Sailor
Coffin Cruises, Head of Rowing and Vulture Repellent

The Ghoul Street Times

COMMUNITY NEWSLETTER

HELP WANTED
Transylvanian language lessons—Knock on Coffin #89 if you can help. I'm going to visit The Olde Country and just need to learn the basics like, "Where is the train station?" "What time does the sun set?" and "Pardon me, but what is your blood type?"

FOR SALE
Fog—I've got way too much of it! Where did all this come from? If you need some, come by Coffin #914 and ask for Misty. Good luck finding the place!

HELP WANTED
Can anyone recommend a good stain remover for teeth? The stuff I'm using works great for grape juice but can't tackle some of the other red beverages I prefer.

Gimme a bang on Coffin #809 if you have any tips on how to improve my smile.

The Ghoul Street Times

Violent New Attraction Exposes HorrorLand's Anti-Vampire Agenda

by Countess Wanda Whiner, Vampire Uncivil Liberties Union

Remember when HorrorLand officials would at least try to hide their anti-vampire sentiments? Well, those days are dead and buried. Has anyone been to the Play Pen recently? There it was—right between the **SNOTBALL TOSS** and **PIN THE TENTACLE ON THE GIANT SQUID**—our own Arcade's latest attraction . . . **VAMPIRE DARTS**!

My horrified brain cannot conceive of a more offensive game! Guests are given an assortment of sharp silver darts to hurl at a distant wall covered in mock Vampire Hearts! **SEND A SILVER DART INTO THE VAMPIRE'S HEART!** reads a nearby sign.

This was the kind of monstrous bullying we came to HorrorLand to escape!

Imagine how the werewolves would howl if the Play Pen opened up a **SILVER BULLET SHOOTING GALLERY**? I demand this newspaper expose this heartbreaking wrongdoing.

Dear Countess Whiner,

You can be assured that we at *The Ghoul Street Times* are also mortified by this repugnant game. We forwarded your complaint and they wrote this letter in return:

Dear Countess Whiner / *The Ghoul Street Times,*

A SILVER BULLET SHOOTING GALLERY is an excellent idea. We'll get right on it!

Faye Vritpasstime
HorrorLand Gaming Council

EYEBALLS, SPIDERS, MIRRORS, AND MORE!

ESCAPE
www.EnterHorrorLand.com

133

Dear Very Special Guest,

From time to time we conduct guest surveys to see how you are enjoying your stay and what you are learning about our amusement park.

Please complete the following survey and leave it at The Crocodile Café. You will receive a complimentary token.

Horrors hate to be pinched.	❏ True	❏ False
Snakes are a Horror's best friend.	❏ True	❏ False
The Ferris Wheel is the Scariest Ride in HorrorLand.	❏ True	❏ False
Dr. Maniac was raised in Werewolf Village.	❏ True	❏ False
Byron's code name is The Keeper.	❏ True	❏ False
There is no 13th floor in The Stagger Inn.	❏ True	❏ False

IT'S A TRAP—
THEY WANT TO SEE
HOW MUCH WE KNOW!

Dearest Very Special Guests,

We're still buried in responses to our last attack of questions, and now we know so much more about each and every one of you. But we're hungry for more information. Please quench our thirst for knowledge by answering the following scary queries:

Q: When checking your room for Horrors, where is the last place you expect to find one?

❑ Under your bed

❑ In your soup

❑ Hanging from your windowsill outside, making bird noises

❑ Crouched in your hamper with your dirty socks

❑ Above you

Q: True or False?

Hairspray is outlawed in Werewolf Village.	❑ True	❑ False
The Doom Slide is alive.	❑ True	❑ False
Horrors make great babysitters.	❑ True	❑ False
There's a maggot in your sneaker.	❑ True	❑ False
The Haunted Theater has no bathroom.	❑ True	❑ False
You are a robot.	❑ True	❑ False

Q: The best way to smash a mirror is:

❑ With a chainsaw.

❑ By sending it to Monster Police Headquarters.

❑ Tie it to a stick and use it as a loud, scary bat-swatter.

❑ Look into it and make your ugliest face.

❑ Head butt.

❑ Hire an opera singer to hit a shrieking high note.

Q: True or False?

Zombie Plaza makes the best Brain Pizza.	❑ True	❑ False
HorrorLand admission is free on your deathday.	❑ True	❑ False
Madame Doom is always right.	❑ True	❑ False
Slapppy the Dummy's voice doesn't echo.	❑ True	❑ False
Santa Claus is a Horror.	❑ True	❑ False
Monster Blood tastes great mixed with milk.	❑ True	❑ False

This last question uses our new Horror Homing Device to read your mind and pinpoint your answer. No need to type a letter or lift a pencil. Simply think about your address ... concentrate on where you are right now. We'll do the rest. . . .

Q: Where are you . . . right now?

DON'T DO IT! THEY'LL FIND YOU!
GO TO WWW.ESCAPEHORRORLAND.COM
FOR MORE LIFE-SAVING ADVICE! FAST!
—LIZZY

T.G. EYE BALLDAY'S

Where we say, "Thank goodness it's EYEBALLS!"

Looking for eyeballs? Well, take a gander at our eye-popping new menu, full to bursting with the finest in Ocular Cuisine! From mild, home-style recipes to spicy eyeballs sure to socket to those taste buds! Roll on down! We'll see you there!

CALIFORNIA BALL
A delicious appet-Eye-zer served sushi-style.
This raw eyeball is wrapped in Goblin Rice and seaweed farmed right from our local Mind Swamp.

CORNEA ON THE COB
Sure, they didn't come that way, but they are so fun to eat!

SLEEPY SEED SALAD
The healthiest Eye-tem on the menu, tossing together Eyes of Newts, Needles, and Prairie Dogs all topped with a giant Elephant Eye Crouton.

JALAPENO PEEPERS
Take off those glasses! This isn't something you eat. We just have one of our Horrors come by and squirt jalapeno juice into your eyes.

THE NAKED EYE
No sauce. No side dishes. Just one big eye looking right at you.

138

EYES CREAM SUNDAE

Don't fill up on Eyeball Entrees! For dessert, we've frozen these eyeballs just right, so they stare out of every scoop as you gobble up the Whipped Aqueous Humor Topping and Smashed Mirror Sprinkles. That little red ball on top, sadly, is not an eyeball . . . it's a maraschino cherry. Gross!

ON THE BALL

Any of our dishes can be topped with one of the following delectable toppings:

CRUSHED IRIS

Not like the flower. Like the part of the eye. (Duh.)

WASAB-EYE

Makes the eyeballs well up right there on your plate!

PEPPERED PUPIL

Ground fresh at your table, causing hours of uninterrupted sneezing.

TEARS

Also comes free with the Wasab-Eye, so most people just order that.

B.Y.O.E.—BRING YOUR OWN EYEBALLS SPECIAL

Some connoisseurs love the way we prepare the eyeballs but wish to bring in a sack, lunch box, or skull full of their own favorites. We encourage this and offer a 20/20 % discount and two complimentary eye patches to those who do!

STICK AROUND THE SPIDER SHACK!
"Come into our Web," said the spiders to . . . YOU!

The Spider Shack may not be large, but it doesn't take much room to
house over a million different spiders. As you'd expect, the interior is
almost entirely covered in webbing. There's not a lot of room in there
but—thanks to that same sticky web—once you're there . . . you're
there to STAY! Luckily, there are plenty of "Arachnitivities":

SEA SPIDER'S SALTY SHANTIES
This grizzled old spider used to sail the swampy seas and he has many
a story and song to share about his watery adventures. There's a
tarantu-lizing tale behind each of his eight peg legs!

DADDY LONGLEG'S HIGH HURDLES
He's an eight-time champion of the Global Pest Olympics; folks marvel
as this nimble racer speeds along in his tiny headband. How can he
possibly do this across the ceiling?

THE BABY SPIDER PARACHUTE TAKE-OFF
They may look as cute as a little fanged button, but make no mistake,
these little monsters are flying toward the horizon with World Spider
Domination on their miniscule young minds.

UNLIMITED WEB ACCESS
No, we don't mean on a computer.

THE BLACK WIDOWS—LIVE!
Ever seen a spider with a Mohawk? Throw your fist in the air (if it's
not webbed to the wall) and cheer as these Spiders of Rock strum
their miniscule guitars—each silkily six-strung with
hard-rock webbing.

MEMO

TO: The Curious
FROM: Cruds Terkel, *Horror Historian*
RE: REFLECTING ON . . . THE HALL OF MIRRORS

Every day, we get a slew of questions about The Hall of Mirrors—that
dangerous, ugly old warthog trap hidden behind all those STAY OUT
signs. (And that barbed wire is alive and poisonous, by the way. Be
careful . . . it's watching.)

All sorts of crazy rumors fly around about that place. Some say it's
gorgeous in there. Pretty, even. Oh, yeah? Look around HorrorLand
and find ANYTHING that's pretty. Not a chance! Others say there are
entrances to other places and dimensions inside. That's ridiculous. The
place is boring, haunted, and covered in broken glass.

HorrorLand shut that place down when Marilyn Medusa, a visiting
Horror supermodel, slithered in and saw her reflection for the first
time. We all knew what she looked like, but, apparently, she had no idea.
She trashed the place, cursed it, and made HorrorLand promise to never
let anyone else ever inside.

I've been in there. I'm not eager to ever go back. You better STAY
OUT of there, too. It's not often that HorrorLand posts a law for the
safety of its guests, so when it does, those laws should be obeyed to
the letter. So stay the Horror out of there!

MORE LIES!

ASK THE HORRORS

It is highly recommended that you never directly ask Horrors any questions. It makes them grumpy and hungry. Instead, HorrorLand is covered with "Ask the Horrors" boxes for our guests to deposit any queries they'd like answered safely:

Q: How do you keep your hair so blue and bushy?

A: The truth is we're just born this good-looking. Don't take it hard, but us Horrors talk behind your backs about how ugly human hair can be—all shiny waves and flowing curls. There's just not much you're going to be able to do with that.

Try not washing it! Let the natural oils do their best. Or, better yet, throw away those combs and barrettes and just use big, fat, gooey slugs. A slug will stick right to the side of your head—you can use it all day—and it never stops oozing. Perfect.

Q: How do I get the guy I like to notice me?

A: I'd throw a rock at him. Boy Horrors like a Girl Horror with a strong throwing arm and good aim. On our first date, I'd always be sure to take any presents he brought me and throw them hard and far into the nearest sludge river to show him I love him.

Q: My parents are always in my business. You Horrors never seem to have to deal with that kind of pressure. What's your secret?

A: Don't look at me. I wasn't really "born" to "parents." I crawled out of a radioactive slime puddle after a witch cursed it. Slime puddles don't make you do chores. Witches, though mean, will let you stay up as late as you want.

Q: Where is Mr. Fuzzy Patches?

A: You mean that adorable little tabby cat somebody left in the lobby of The Stagger Inn? It was delic—I mean, adorable. I haven't seen it lately. (Burp).

The Deadly Daily

GHASTLY GOSSIP

HorrorLand is abuzz with rumors surrounding our new Gift Shop that's soon to open. Until now, we've known nothing about the mysterious stranger who's running the place, but Ghastly Gossip has just learned that his name is . . . **JONATHAN CHILLER**.

HorrorLand
WEREWOLF VILLAGE

ENJOY A HAIR-RAISING HIKE IN WOLFSBANE FOREST.

GO WILD AT THE ALL-NEW WEREWOLF PETTING ZOO.

AND LAST BUT NOT LEASHED... DON'T MISS OUR "SUNRISE SPECIAL". WEREWOLVES EAT FUR FREE!

Spend One Day at HorrorLand and You'll Never Be the Same.
www.EnterHorrorLand.com

Here are some other rumors that we've heard about this new establishment:

"See how fast that place is getting built? He can't possibly have less than nine arms."

"His knickknacks are out of this world. I'm going to buy one of everything."

"He used to run a gift shop in the Six Hags Amusement Park. He gave away free souvenirs! But there was a catch . . . I can't quite remember what it was. . . ."

So is he single? Is he a werewolf? A squid? A HUMAN?!? (Yuk! Scandalous!) The truth is we have no idea. All we know is that this Jonathan Chiller is hard at work on the shop's construction. Hammering, screams, and gurgles blast from behind its still-locked doors day and night. So stay alert and check back with Ghastly Gossip in the future for more on this peculiar new citizen of HorrorLand. . . .

BEHIND THE SCREAMS

BEHIND THE SCREAMS

CONTENTS

Bonus material written and compiled by Matthew D. Payne

FRIGHT GALLERY

SLAPPY THE DUMMY

FIRST APPEARANCE *Night of the Living Dummy*

OTHER APPEARANCES *Night of the Living Dummy II* and *III*; Goosebumps 2000: *Bride of the Living Dummy*; Goosebumps 2000: *Slappy's Nightmare*; Goosebumps HorrorLand #1: *Revenge of the Living Dummy*

NICKNAMES
Ol' Crazy Eyes
The BAAAAD Boy
The Dummy That Is No Dummy

SMOOTHEST MOVES Some people believe that Slappy has the power to control people's minds and turn *people* into puppets.

WEAKNESS *"Karru marri odonna loma molonu karrano."* Those six words have an eerie and often surprising effect on dummies.

LIVING or DEAD? Both!

TIE or BOWTIE? Definitely bowtie!

FAVORITE MOVIE *Dumb and Dumber* (the only two labels he ever gives his human slaves)

FAVORITE FOOD He never has to eat—he's a dummy!

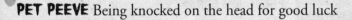

PET PEEVE Being knocked on the head for good luck

BIGGEST FEAR Termites

PETS Slappy thinks the entire human race is his plaything.

DISTANT COUSIN Pinocchio

HOBBIES Thinking up the worst insult possible

WORST INSULTS
Is that a mustache, or are you eating a rat?
Hey—you're pretty. Pretty ugly!
I've seen PIMPLES that were prettier than you!

LAST SEEN Wreaking havoc in **www.EnterHorrorLand.com**

SPLAT STATS

STRENGTH	✸ ✸ ✸ ✸ ✸
INTELLIGENCE	✸ ✸ ✸ ✸ ✸ ✸ ✸ ✸
SPEED	✸ ✸ ✸ ✸ ✸ ✸
ATTACK SKILLS	✸ ✸ ✸ ✸ ✸ ✸ ✸
HUMOR	✸ ✸ ✸ ✸ ✸ ✸ ✸ ✸
EVIL	✸ ✸ ✸ ✸ ✸ ✸ ✸ ✸ ✸
SPLINTERS	✸ ✸ ✸ ✸ ✸ ✸ ✸ ✸ ✸

FRIGHT GALLERY

LONG BEN ONE-LEG

FIRST APPEARANCE Goosebumps HorrorLand #2: *Creep from the Deep*

NICKAMES
Captain Ben
Ol' Ben
Scourge of the South Sea

GREATEST ASSET His crew of rotten but loyal zombie pirates

WEAKNESS He can't swim.

LIVING or DEAD Dead . . . for 200 years!

PRIZED POSSESSION His long black coat—his tailor wasn't lying when he said it would last forever!

COFFEE or TEA Neither . . . he prefers straight saltwater.

FAVORITE FOOD Pillaged food always tastes better.

FAVORITE SEASICKNESS REMEDY Two yellow sea slugs with a dash of rat guts

FAVORITE MUSIC Irish sea chanteys

HOBBIES Collecting maggots; chess

FAVORITE VACATION SPOT Davy Jones's Locker

BIGGEST BOOTY 5,000 Spanish silver coins plundered off the coast of Portugal

CLASSIC QUOTES

Captain Ben asks *the questions and he* answers *the questions.*

Being dead for over 200 years has put Captain Ben in a very bad mood.

Show them what we call pirate mercy!

I WANT MY LEG!

LAST SEEN In Map 2 of **www.EnterHorrorLand.com**

SPLAT STATS

STRENGTH	●	●	●	●	●	●	●			
INTELLIGENCE	●	●	●	●	●	●	●	●	●	
SPEED	●	●	●							
ATTACK SKILLS	●	●	●	●	●	●				
HUMOR	●	●	●	●	●	●				
EVIL	●	●	●	●	●					
SCURVY	●	●	●	●	●	●	●	●	●	●

FRIGHT GALLERY

PURPLE RAGE

FIRST APPEARANCE Goosebumps HorrorLand #5: *Dr. Maniac vs. Robby Schwartz*

OTHER APPEARANCES Please, no more. Please?

NICKNAMES
The Rage
Mr. Angry
Violet Riot
The World's Best-Looking Supervillain

SMOOTHEST MOVES Able to bend metal poles and punch holes into walls with ease. Can fly like Superman. A very angry Superman.

WEAKNESS Will explode in anger if laughed at

ARCHENEMIES Dr. Maniac and the Scarlet Starlet

PARTNERS IN CRIME Nobody. The Purple Rage works alone.

FAVORITE COLOR Take a guess.

COFFEE or TEA? Coffee

FAVORITE FOOD Burnt toast

FAVORITE MOVIE *12 Angry Men*

HOBBIES Perfecting his hairdo; polishing his purple boots; reorganizing his closet of purple capes; yoga

PETS None, but he keeps several houseplants. Many of them are dying, which makes the Purple Rage—you guessed it—angry.

FAVORITE MUSIC Thrash Metal

FAVORITE THINGS TO SAY WHEN ANGRY
Know what really PADDLES my PANCAKES?
Know what really HONKS my HORSE?
This really GRIPES my GOATEE!
Know what really BITES my GIRAFFE?

LAST SEEN In Map 10 of **www.EnterHorrorLand.com**

SPLAT STATS

STRENGTH	●	●	●	●	●	●	●	●		
INTELLIGENCE	●	●	●	●	●	●	●			
SPEED	●	●	●	●	●	●				
ATTACK SKILLS	●	●	●	●	●					
HUMOR	●	●	●	●	●	●	●	●		
EVIL	●	●	●							
BLOOD PRESSURE	●	●	●	●	●	●	●	●	●	●	●

FRIGHT GALLERY

KING TUTTAN-RAH

FIRST APPEARANCE Goosebumps HorrorLand #6: *Who's Your Mummy?*

NICKNAMES
Organ Grinder
Not Uncle Jonathan
His Royally Crazy Highness

GREATEST ASSET An army of bats ready to tear his enemies to shreds

PARTNERS IN CRIME Sonja and Annie

PARTNER IN CRIME WHO IS ALSO A PET Cleopatra the Cat

WEAKNESS Water

LIVING or DEAD Dead

COFFEE or TEA Tea, with a splash of mummy stomach acid

RECOMMENDED RECIPES
Broiled Heart of Mummy with Béarnaise Sauce
Chopped Liver of Mummy with Onions
Mummy Sausage: Spiced Ground Mummy Kidney in Intestinal
    Casing
Frozen Lung Pops

FAVORITE GAME Operation

DISTANT COUSIN Prince Khor-Ru

FAVORITE MOVIE *The Mummy* (I mean, did you really have to ask?)

HOBBIES Collecting hair; collecting mummies; writing haikus

LAST SEEN In Map 6 of **www.EnterHorrorLand.com**

SPLAT STATS

STRENGTH	✦✦✦✦✦✦✦✦
INTELLIGENCE	✦✦✦✦✦✦✦✦
SPEED	✦✦✦✦✦
ATTACK SKILLS	✦✦✦✦✦✦
HUMOR	✦✦✦✦✦
EVIL	✦✦✦✦✦✦✦
IMPERSONATION SKILLS	✦✦✦✦✦✦✦✦✦✦

FRIGHT GALLERY

INSPECTOR CRANIUM

FIRST APPEARANCE Goosebumps HorrorLand #10: *Help! We Have Strange Powers!*

NICKNAME The Brain Drain

ACTUAL NAME Too hard to pronounce

WORKS FOR The Institute

MEMBER OF The Thought Police

SMOOTHEST MOVE Forcing his way into people's minds

TRUSTY ASSISTANT Finney

WEAKNESS Underestimating brainy kids

LIVING or DEAD Living

COFFEE or TEA Decaffeinated coffee

PETS Two lab rats by the names of Salt and Pepper

FAVORITE GAME Trivial Pursuit

FAVORITE MUSIC Silence

PET PEEVE Superheroes

CLASSIC QUOTES
The Institute doesn't make mistakes.
I have to drain your brains!

LAST SEEN In Map 10 of **www.EnterHorrorLand.com**

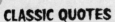

──── SPLAT STATS ────

STRENGTH	
INTELLIGENCE	
SPEED	
ATTACK SKILLS	
HUMOR	
EVIL	
MIND CONTROL	

TRICKS AND TIPS
FOR HORRORLAND GAMING!

Want to scare your friends with your amazing Goosebumps game skills? Try these tips the next time you set out to dominate the playing field at www.enterhorrorland.com and Goosebumps HorrorLand: The Video Game.

www.EnterHorrorLand.com

CONSULT MADAME DOOM anytime you're lost or stumped.
Click either her booth on any map or her icon in the menu.

A QUICK CLICK on the "Boorista" behind the counter of the Café in Map 3 will earn you some of the corniest jokes in HorrorLand.

While you're at the Café, SNOOP AROUND the room to see what other freaky features you can find.

You'll only be able to SURROUND THE PESKY MONSTER PETS in Map 4 with five discs if you start putting discs down BEFORE they stop moving to the next spot. You just have to predict when and where they're going to stop.

Avoid your doom on the Doom Slide in Map 10 by paying very close attention to the NUMBERS that appear BEHIND THE SKULLS at the very start of each section. If you miss which numbers are where, you'll never make it!

If you're ever baffled by a game, you'll be given the option to win a game of FIND THE EYEBALL to skip it. Unfortunately, you can't skip both levels.

In Map 9's Bat Barn, make sure you aim BEFORE you fire! If you hold down the fire button, you won't be able to move!

GOOSEBUMPS HORRORLAND:
THE VIDEO GAME

Visit the INFORMATION BOOTH in Carnival of Screams to receive important park info—and a very SPECIAL GIFT!

Once you've unlocked Vampire Village, you can get your kicks playing games there AND go back to Carnival of Screams to play games and EARN MORE FRIGHTS. Awesome!

The GLOWING RED EYES in Roller Ghoster aren't there to watch your pretty face go by. SHOOT THEM FOR POINTS! Pow!

Need a hint? Chat up the FORTUNE-TELLER in Carnival of Screams or Vampire Village.

Need a laugh? Pick up one of the phones in Vampire Village to hear a frightfully funny VAMPIRE JOKE.

If you can handle the gross factor, pull the slug's tongue in Rub-a-Dub Slug to reveal 10 hidden tokens. Ka-ching!

Check out the "Behind the Screams" feature in Goosebumps: *One Day in HorrorLand* for even more clues—including one on how to win the BONUS MONSTER CARD!

For more tips and a behind-the-scenes peek at the video game, visit
www.goosebumpsvideogame.com

GOOSEBUMPS ON THE WEB!

Have you checked out every corner of the Goosebumps universe?
Take a look at the quick stats of three key sites you should
explore for more, more, MORE!!!

 ## GOOSEBUMPS: THE OFFICIAL SITE
www.scholastic.com/goosebumps/

WHY YOU GOTTA GO

It's overflowing with information on all things Goosebumps! This is the
OFFICIAL SITE of everyone's favorite scary series—the one that has
sold more than 300 million copies in 32 languages worldwide! At this site,
fear seekers can catch up on the latest Goosebumps news, watch clips of
Goosebumps DVDs, and interact with other fright fans!

DID YOU KNOW?

Think you know everything there is to know about R.L. Stine's series? Test
your knowledge by playing the TRIVIA GAME in the GAMES section. Find out
which of your friends knows the most.

DON'T MISS

Participate in the creation of a BRAND-NEW Goosebumps tale along with
fellow readers by clicking on CHAIN STORY in the GAMES section.

GOOSEBUMPS HORRORLAND: ENTER HORRORLAND
www.enterhorrorland.com

WHY YOU GOTTA GO
The famous scream park comes alive (along with your nightmares) at this wild website. There are 12 Maps of attractions featuring the villains you love to hate (like Slappy the Dummy and Dr. Maniac), gut-busting games, and terrifying trivia.

DID YOU KNOW?
Over 600,000 gamers have registered at the website. Considering each registered user screams at least 10 times while exploring the site, then the website has caused over 6 million screams and counting!!!

DON'T MISS
Make your own monster and share it with other gamers in the Café.

GOOSEBUMPS HORRORLAND: THE VIDEO GAME
www.goosebumpsvideogame.com

WHY YOU GOTTA GO
This site contains EVERYTHING you'd want to know about the Goosebumps HorrorLand Video Game. Look at "screamshots," watch video clips from the game, learn more about all of the Horrors you'll meet (and run from) in the game, and download wallpaper and buddy icons!

DID YOU KNOW?
If you think you've seen it all, think again! The video game is a little different from the Goosebumps HorrorLand books with even creepier Horrors like the Vampire Horror and Clown Horror!

DON'T MISS
Download Tips and Tricks for the video game in the Mad Labs section of the site!

MAKE YOUR OWN
HAUNTED MASK

Ready to scare the wits out of your friends on Halloween?! Want the fright of The Haunted Mask but be able to take it off when you're through spooking? Then try this creepy and crafty activity!

WARNING
This activity is too tough to do on your own—grab a parent and ask for his or her help. This could get messy: lay paper on the floor underneath you and wear clothes that can get dirty.

Supplies Needed
Plaster cloth or plaster bandages
Vaseline
Plastic wrap
Paint, markers, yarn, buttons, crafty objects, etc.
Stapler or Crazy Glue

Instructions
1. Cut the plaster cloth or plaster bandages (which can be found easily online but may also be at your local drug store, medical supply store, or arts and crafts store) into 1 x 4-inch-long strips.

2. Apply Vaseline over your entire face. Have an adult cover your hair with plastic wrap and then cover the plastic with Vaseline. Make sure the plastic covers only your hair and is not on your skin. Lean back in a chair so you face the ceiling.

3. Have an adult dip the strips into water and mold them onto your face, strip by strip, making sure to mold the strips tightly to your face and tightly together. (Leave openings around your eyes, nostrils, and mouth so you can see and breathe!)

4. Build 3 layers onto your face with the plaster cloth or plaster bandages.

5. Let the mask dry on your face for about 20 minutes. This may be a good time to sing Halloween favorites like the Addams Family theme or "The Monster Mash" to pass the time.

6. Make funny faces to loosen the mask from your face, then have your adult helper peel the mask off slowly and carefully.

7. Let the mask dry overnight.

8. The next day, cut additional strips of plaster cloth or plaster bandages, dip them in water, and add them to the mask to create funny features. Build a crazy-looking nose, give yourself huge ears, horns, or a long tongue. Remember to build up a few layers to make it strong, then let it dry overnight again.

9. Add character to your mask! Paint it with poster, acrylic, or polyurethane paint. Use markers to add creepy details: warts, scars, etc. Glue strips of yarn for hair. Use your imagination and don't forget to fright!

10. Staple or Crazy Glue yarn to either side of the inside of the mask at ear level. Have an adult help you tie and tighten the strings behind your head so it's tight enough to sit on your ears and keep the mask on, but not tight enough to make it hard for you to take off. Remember, you don't want to suffer the same fate as Carly Beth!

MEET THE HORRORLAND MANAGEMENT

Scaring helpless children isn't easy. It takes years of education in the Art of Fright, not to mention endless hours of on-the-job training. We at HorrorLand realize that you, our honored guests, came here to scream until you can no longer speak, which is why we handpick the most frightening employees possible. Our Horrors are known across the world for their ability to haunt, taunt, and generally freak out our guests. But the biggest thanks must be given to our management team—simply the worst in the business. Here's some more information on key members of our group.

RUSTY BOLTZ, Director of Rides and Entertainment

Mr. Boltz received several technical degrees from the Frankenstein Institute of Technology. He currently holds the world record for most screams per second heard coming from a theme park ride.

DI KWICKLEY, Head of Guest Relations

Mr. Kwickly is always ready with a smile to ignore requests and complaints from guests. A leader in his field, he also works with a number of organizations, including the International Say-One-Thing-But-Do-Another Association.

EARL E. GRAVE & PEARL E. Gates, Innkeepers

Mr. Grave and Ms. Gates know that it is the little things that make a guest happy, which is why they make sure skeletons appear in every closet and bedbugs fill every mattress.

CHEF HENRI GURGITATE, Manager of Food and Stink

Chef Gurgitate studied at some of the finest culinary institutes in Transylvania and came to America (and HorrorLand) with expertise in rotten flesh, cauldron pressure-cooking, and rare slime spices. He learned new flavoring techniques catering for zombies, a true feat considering how bland brains are.

DOUG HISGRAVE, VP of Park Operations

Mr. Hisgrave assures that HorrorLand runs as smoothly as possible. He comes from a Cemetery Management background, which makes him a perfect fit for our theme park!

The World's
Maddest Scientists

Dr. Maniac is just one of many mad scientists. It seems that the world is filled with crazed chemists, batty biologists, and freaky physicists. Check out the chart below to see how Dr. Maniac compares with a few of the craziest.

SCIENTIST	AREAS OF EXPERTISE	CRAZIEST INVENTION	FAVORITE FOOD	FAVORITE VACATION SPOT
Dr. Twisted, from Goosebumps HorrorLand #3: *Monster Blood for Breakfast*	monster biology / fluid composition	a powerful new strain of Monster Blood	split pea soup	HorrorLand Theme Park
Dr. Jekyll, from *Dr. Jekyll & Mr. Hyde*	organic chemistry / schizophrenia	Mr. Hyde, his evil side	Dr. Jekyll likes angel food cake. Mr. Hyde likes devil's food cake.	Dr. Jekyll prefers the Caribbean, while Mr. Hyde enjoys dark alleyways.
Dr. Maniac, from Goosebumps HorrorLand #5: *Dr. Maniac vs. Robby Schwartz*	scream therapy	Dr. Maniac's World of Pain	mixed nuts	the Bermuda Triangle
Dr. Frankenstein, from *Frankenstein*	sewing / electrical engineering	Frankenstein's Monster	microwaved leftovers	the Transylvanian mountains
Dr. Griffin, from *The Invisible Man*	particle physics / eavesdropping	invisibility formula	fresh fruit and vegetables (all invisible, of course)	unsure: nobody has ever spotted him
Dr. Fredericks, from Goosebumps: *Say Cheese and Die!*	photography / cheating	technically nothing—he stole all his ideas	day-old bread	his basement

There's No Escaping the Horror

You may be through with *Welcome to Horrorland: A Survival Guide*, but HorrorLand's not through with YOU.

Step right up and meet Murder the Clown, Jonathan Chiller, and find out what happens

WHEN THE GHOST DOG HOWLS

"Andy, trade popcorn bags with me," Marnie said. She made a grab for my bag.

I swiped it away from her and spilled popcorn all over my lap. "Marnie — give me a break," I said with a groan. "Why do you want mine?"

"Yours looks like it tastes better," she said.

"Huh?" I squinted into my popcorn bag. "They're exactly the same."

"Then you don't mind trading — right?" She laughed.

My cousin, Marnie Myers, may be the grabbiest person in the world. And she always wants everything that's mine. But at least she has a sense of humor.

I like her laugh. She's twelve, the same age as me. But she laughs like a little kid.

She *looks* younger than me, too. In fact, even though we're cousins, we don't look anything alike.

She's short and thin. She has a narrow face with straight brown hair down to her shoulders and big green eyes.

Dad says I could be a middle linebacker. I guess that's his polite way of saying I'm big and maybe a little chubby. I have a round face with short black hair and brown eyes.

Dad says I always have a worried look. I don't think he's right. But yes, kids are always asking me, "Hey, Andy, what's wrong?" when nothing is wrong.

Marnie and I get along really well — except when she's grabbing my popcorn or taking handfuls of French fries off my plate at lunch.

I handed her my popcorn. "Well? Aren't you going to give me yours?"

She shoved my hand away. "I have to taste them both first."

We were in HorrorLand Theme Park, sitting in the Haunted Theater, waiting for the show to start. The theater looked like a creepy, old haunted house in a horror movie.

The auditorium was dark, except for flickering candles on the walls. Thick cobwebs hung down from the balcony. Creepy organ music played. A skeleton usher stood in the aisle, holding a flashlight.

Suddenly, jagged lightning bolts flashed on the black curtain across the stage. And thunder boomed over the auditorium.

Behind us, a little kid started to cry. "This is *too scary*!" he wailed. "I don't *like* it!" His parents stood up, pulled him to the aisle, and led him out.

Marnie and I laughed. We'd been having good, scary fun all week in HorrorLand. Especially since our parents let us go off on our own most of the time.

Some of the rides were terrifying. And we both screamed our heads off in Werewolf Village. The half-human, half-wolf creatures were so *real*! Were they men wearing hairy costumes? The way they growled and snapped their pointed teeth, you'd *swear* you were staring at the real thing!

And another of our favorite places was The Game Preserve. Miles and miles of video games. Of course, Marnie had to play until she beat me at every game.

And now here we were, in the third row of the Haunted Theater, waiting for the show to start. In dripping green letters, a sign over the stage read: GHOST TOWN CLOWN SHOW.

Storm sounds poured out of the loudspeakers. Lightning flashed. Thunder boomed.

And I gasped as someone grabbed my shoulder and squeezed it hard.

"Hey!" I stared up into the face of a grinning clown standing in the aisle. He leaned over me and squeezed my shoulder again.

The clown's face was caked in white makeup.

His painted grin was crooked and smeared. He had a red bulb for a nose. A red-and-blue ruffled collar around his neck.

And as he leaned over me, I saw a hatchet buried deep in the top of his bald head. The blade was halfway in his skull. The handle poked up at an angle. Painted blood trickled down both sides of his face.

"Hiya, kid," he growled in a hoarse voice. "Let me introduce myself to ya. I'm Murder the Clown."

My mouth hung open. I wanted to say something, but I was too startled.

His breath smelled like onions. He brought his face down close to mine. And I could see that his eyes were totally bloodshot. And there were cracks all over his white makeup.

"Hey, kid — know why they call me Murder the Clown?" he growled.

"Because you have a hatchet in your head?" I answered.

His eyes bulged in shock. "I have a *what*?" he cried. "You're *joking*!"

Of course he was being funny. So I laughed.

But he squeezed my arm and jerked me to my feet. "Come on, kid. Enough of this. You're outta here." He began to pull me to the stage.

I tried to pull back, but he was very strong. "Huh? What did *I* do?" I cried. "Hey — let go! Where are you *taking* me?"

Thunder crashed, shaking the auditorium. In the flicker of a lightning flash, I saw faces in the audience staring at the big clown and me. Behind me, Marnie jumped to her feet and made her way toward us.

"Come on, kiddo," Murder growled. "You've been volunteered." He raised both white-gloved hands to my shoulders and pushed me up the aisle.

I slid out from under his grasp. "I've been *what?*"

"You've been volunteered to be in the show," he said. "Fun time. You'll love it. Maybe you'll win a prize. What size clown costume do you wear? Are you a medium or a large? You're pretty big. I think I have an extra large back there."

"Wait a minute!" Marnie grabbed Murder by the collar. "Why does *Andy* get to be in it? I want to be in it, too."

Murder turned his watery, red eyes on my cousin. "I like you," he rasped. "I think I have a big nose that will fit you."

He gave us both a push. "Come on. We don't want to make the zombie clowns late for their meal. Know what they're having for lunch today?"

"No. What?" I asked.

"YOU!"

I didn't want to do this. No way. I'm kind of shy. Marnie was a *lot* more excited about going onstage than I was.

But a few minutes later, there we were in our red-and-white polka dot clown costumes. I had a big pillow tucked in my front to make me look fat and a stiff yellow wig that stood straight up in the air like a broom.

Marnie wore enormous platform boots that made her about eight feet tall. She had an ugly red smile smeared over her white face. She wore puffy yellow overalls over a bright green shirt, with a red ruffled collar. A pointy red-striped hat tilted on her head like a dunce cap.

"Break a leg!" Murder whispered. He raised his big gloved hands and shoved us out onto the stage.

The show had already started. The lights were dim. Creepy music played. A ghostly fog billowed all over the stage.

Scary-looking clowns in drab black-and-gray costumes were doing handstands and somersaults in the fog. Marnie and I were the only ones wearing bright colors.

As I stumbled onstage, I saw a clown with a skull instead of a face. His ugly clown smile was painted in bright red lipstick on the skull. Beside him, I saw a sad-looking clown dressed in rags. He kept moaning and pulling out hunks of his curly hair.

The audience cheered as the clowns started to juggle. What were they throwing back and forth? It was hard to see in the fog. Were those shrunken heads they were tossing?

The clown with the skeleton face pulled Marnie and me into the circle of ghost clowns. Someone tossed me a shrunken head. "That's my Uncle Herman!" he shouted. "Toss him back!"

The head felt soft and warm. I tossed it back to the clown. Soon, Marnie and I were tossing the heads around with the other clowns. Faster and faster, till the audience cheered.

"You're doing great, kids," Murder the Clown called from the side of the stage.

But then I saw something that made me gasp. And that moment is where the fun ended — and the terror began.

In front of the stage, a fat clown was waving his hands at the audience. Suddenly, his hands vanished, and he waved with bony stubs. Then the hands returned. Then just fingers floated on the ends of his arms.

As I stared, the hands kept appearing and disappearing. Was the fog playing tricks on my eyes?

I turned to see what Marnie was doing — and saw a bald clown with sad, black eyes lift his head off his neck. He tossed it across the stage to another clown.

"Hey —" I let out a cry. I gaped at the clown's stub of a neck poking up from his ruffled collar.

The second clown tossed the head in the air — and it floated above the stage. It bobbed high above us and didn't come down.

My heart started to pound.

Is this really happening?

Marnie put her hand on my shoulder. "Relax, Andy," she said. "It's all just part of the show."

"But — but —" I pointed to the headless clown.

The lights came on in the theater. I turned and squinted at the audience.

"Oh, wow," I murmured. "Marnie — look!" I grabbed my cousin by the shoulders and pointed.

When we were sitting out there, the theater had been filled with normal people. Kids and families.

But now, some of the people in the audience looked like creatures from a horror movie!

I saw rotting faces with missing eyeballs. . . . Heads with patches of hair torn away and bare skull poking out at the top . . . Missing arms . . . Open, toothless mouths with thick gobs of drool pouring over decayed chins . . . Shirts torn open and bloody guts dangling down.

"They look like GHOULS!" I cried. "Ghouls and zombies!"

And as I stared, the ugly creatures pulled themselves to their feet. And began to push their way into the aisles.

People screamed. Kids were crying. Some of the normal people grabbed their belongings and hurried to leave.

The auditorium filled with frightening moans and groans. The ugly creatures staggered toward the stage, eyes shut, arms stretched stiffly in front of them.

Marnie and I froze, watching in terror as the ghouls lumbered toward us.

I stared into the dark, empty eye sockets of a grinning skull — a ghoulish woman, covered in crawling spiders. She tore out clumps of her hair as she staggered toward us.

"NOOOO!" I spun away. My eyes swept over the empty stage. "Marnie — the clowns! They all disappeared!"

Marnie and I were alone up there.

Bony green hands grabbed the edge of the stage. And then one of the creatures swung himself up. Groaning, moaning, they were all hoisting themselves onto the stage.

Holding onto my cousin, I took a trembling step back.

And heard the frightened voice of Murder the Clown from somewhere backstage.

"Malfunction! Malfunction!" he screamed. "Something is WRONG! Can't anyone SHUT THEM DOWN? The zombies are *out of control*!"

His terrified cry sent a chill down my body. I could tell it wasn't an act. The clown was really afraid!

More ghoulish creatures climbed onto the stage. Their heavy shoes scraped the floor. They moaned as if they were in pain.

As they staggered forward, their eyes were locked on Marnie and me. Their hands were outstretched, reaching for us.

We took another step back. I gazed around frantically. "Marnie — the stage door!"

We both took off toward the back wall. A narrow wooden door stood in the corner.

I grabbed the handle. Twisted it and pulled.

"It — it's LOCKED!" I cried.

COME FAMILIES! COME FRIENDS! TO A PLACE THAT'S GRAND! FOR FUN AND THRILLS, VISIT HORRORLAND!

WITH TWISTS AND TURNS AND FLIPS AND SPINS! OUR RIDES ARE A RIOT! SO STRAP YOURSELF IN!

IF YOUR TUMMY IS GRUMBLY, PLEASE DON'T BE SHY! WE'VE GOT OODLES OF TREATS TO TRY!

SO COME FOR ADVENTURE AND FANTASY TOO! YOUR HORRORLAND FRIENDS WILL BE WAITING FOR YOU!

Read the books. Play the games.
Defeat the Dummy.
www.EnterHorrorLand.com

ENTERHL

◼ SCHOLASTIC

PLACE ON EARTH!

The Original Bone-Chilling

Series

NIGHT of the LIVING DUMMY

R.L. STINE

DEEP TROUBLE

R.L. STINE

MONSTER BLOOD

R.L. STINE

The HAUNTED MASK

R.L. STINE

ONE DAY at HORRORLAND

R.L. STINE

the CURSE of the MUMMY'S TOMB

R.L. STINE

Now with all-new bonus material—splat stats and more!

NEED MORE THRILLS?

Get Goosebumps!

PLAY

Wii — Goosebumps HORRORLAND

PlayStation 2 — Goosebumps HORRORLAND

Nintendo DS — Goosebumps HORRORLAND

WATCH

R.L. STINE — Goosebumps A NIGHT IN TERROR TOWER

R.L. STINE — Goosebumps ONE DAY AT HORRORLAND

R.L. STINE — Goosebumps MONSTER BLOOD

LISTEN

Goosebumps HorrorLand

THE LIVING DUMMY
R.L. STINE

Goosebumps HorrorLand
DISC 1
REVENGE OF THE LIVING DUMMY
R.L. STINE

Goosebumps HorrorLand

CREEP FROM THE DEEP
R.L. STINE

Goosebumps HorrorLand
DISC 1
CREEP FROM THE DEEP
R.L. STINE